"I think I feel my baby."

Ashley lifted her gaze to Jarrett's, amazed by the sensations inside her.

Eyes widening, Jarrett's gaze dropped to her stomach. "Is this the first time? How does it feel?"

"Like bubbles. Here." Without pausing to think, she took his hand and guided it under her T-shirt, low on her belly. His broad palm and long fingers were warm against the thin knit of her shorts. Beneath them, Ashley felt her baby's tiny, fluttering movements.

"It's going crazy in there," she said. "All day long I've had this funny tingling feeling, but I didn't think...it didn't occur to me that it was my baby."

Suddenly Ashley realized how naturally she had placed Jarrett's hand on her, how intimately his fingers were still splayed across her stomach, over her child. She wanted to move away. Yet she didn't want to move.

Except perhaps to get closer to Jarrett...

Dear Reader,

Special Edition is pleased to bring you six exciting love stories to help you celebrate spring...and blossoming love.

To start off the month, don't miss *A Father for Her Baby* by Celeste Hamilton—a THAT'S MY BABY! title that features a pregnant amnesiac who is reunited with her long-ago fiancé. Now she must uncover the past in order to have a future with this irresistible hero and her new baby.

April offers Western romances aplenty! In the third installment of her action-packed HEARTS OF WYOMING series, Myrna Temte delivers *Wrangler.* A reticent lady wrangler has a mighty big secret, but sparks fly between her and the sexy lawman she's been trying very hard to avoid; the fourth book in the series will be available in July. Next, Pamela Toth brings us another heartwarming story in her popular BUCKLES & BRONCOS miniseries. In *Buchanan's Pride,* a feisty cowgirl rescues a stranded stranger—only to discover he's the last man on earth she should let into her heart!

There's more love on the range coming your way. *Finally His Bride* by Christine Flynn—part of THE WHITAKER BRIDES series—is an emotional reunion romance between two former sweethearts. Also the MEN OF THE DOUBLE-C RANCH series continues when a brooding Clay brother claims the woman he's never stopped wanting in *A Wedding For Maggie* by Allison Leigh. Finally, debut author Carol Finch shares an engaging story about a fun-loving rodeo cowboy who woos a romance-resistant single mom in *Not Just Another Cowboy.*

I hope you enjoy these stirring tales of passion, and each and every romance to come!

Sincerely,

Karen Taylor Richman
Senior Editor

Please address questions and book requests to:
Silhouette Reader Service
U.S.: 3010 Walden Ave., P.O. Box 1325, Buffalo, NY 14269
Canadian: P.O. Box 609, Fort Erie, Ont. L2A 5X3

CELESTE HAMILTON

A FATHER
FOR HER BABY

SPECIAL EDITION®

Published by Silhouette Books
America's Publisher of Contemporary Romance

12080396

For my editor, Lynda Curnyn,
who never gave up on this book.
Thank you, Lynda.

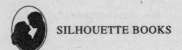 SILHOUETTE BOOKS

ISBN 0-373-24237-9

A FATHER FOR HER BABY

This edition published by arrangement with Harlequin Books S.A.

® and TM are trademarks of Harlequin Books S.A., used under license.
Trademarks indicated with ® are registered in the United States Patent
and Trademark Office, the Canadian Trade Marks Office and in other
countries.

Printed in U.S.A.

CELESTE HAMILTON

has been writing since she was ten years old, with the encouragement of parents who told her she could do anything she set out to do and teachers who helped her refine her talents.

The broadcast media captured her interest in high school, and she graduated from the University of Tennessee with a B.S. in Communications. From there, she began writing and producing commercials at a Chattanooga, Tennessee, radio station.

Celeste began writing romances in 1985 and now works at her craft full-time. Married to a policeman, she likes nothing better than spending time at home with him and their two much-loved cats, although she and her husband also enjoy traveling when their busy schedules permit. Wherever they go, however, "It's always nice to come home to East Tennessee—one of the most beautiful corners of the world."

Dear Reader,

Perhaps no other event inspires the same complex range of emotions as the anticipated birth of a child. Joy mixes with fear, excitement with anxiety. A baby is a symbol of hope and possible dreams. A baby both transforms and complicates the life of the parents. With such rich emotions at play, no wonder pregnancy and babies are such popular components of romance fiction.

Because I love writing about families, I've created my share of fictional babies. But no child has ever presented me with the challenges of the one carried by Ashley Grant, heroine of this book.

First, Ashley is missing from her family. When she's found, she doesn't know her name, her personal history or even the father of the baby she is due to deliver in six months. No man steps forward. Enter Dr. Jarrett McMullen, Ashley's first love, a man who is at once familiar and yet a total stranger. Jarrett is unquestionably *not* her baby's father, but the attraction between them is immediate and intense. Jarrett, truly a special man, wants both Ashley and her child in his life. But Ashley, a woman unsure of her own identity, must be certain she is loved for herself, not for the sake of her child and not for the woman she was before she left home.

The tangled emotions and needs of these characters made my job as a writer interesting. What kept the story moving was the baby Ashley carried—an innocent, precious child. A child who deserved the loving family Ashley and Jarrett could create if they would just trust their hearts.

Children are our collective hope for the future. That's why writing and reading "baby" stories is such a positive experience. I certainly hope *A Father for Her Baby* leaves you smiling and feeling good about this miracle we call life.

Happy reading!

Celeste Hamilton

Prologue

Today she would be married.
She would become Mrs. Jarrett McMullen.
Dr. Jarrett McMullen's wife.

That sweet, thrilling knowledge made Ashley Grant laugh out loud as she snuggled deeper into the covers. April sunlight streamed through half-closed blinds and highlighted the clock beside the bed. Nearly 9:00 a.m. She had slept in, but she supposed that was allowed for a bride on her wedding day.

Too bad Jarrett hadn't that luxury. By now, he should be off duty at the Dallas hospital where he was a resident. Soon, he would arrive here at his apartment, the home she was going to share with him.

Hopefully, he could catch a few hours of sleep. Then they would steal away to a chapel about an hour's drive from the city, where the minister and his wife were expecting them at two o'clock. Ashley would slip into the wedding dress that was hanging right now over the bedroom door. She would walk down the aisle of the little white church, carrying a bouquet of roses, with the warm Texas spring breeze blowing through the open windows and the wedding march spilling from the piano.

Even without their friends and families to witness the ceremony, Ashley knew her wedding to Jarrett would be perfect, the fulfillment of years of postponed dreams.

The rattle of keys in the living-room door brought her out of her reverie. She pushed her tousled, long blond hair out of her face, scrambled from bed and to the bedroom doorway. Jarrett stood across the living room and sorted through some mail, so he didn't see her at first. Ashley had plenty of time to feast her eyes on the man she had loved for so long.

He had obviously grabbed a shower at the hospital and changed out of his more professional attire into casual clothes—a faded denim shirt and an ancient pair of jeans. Jarrett wore jeans exceedingly well. They rode low on his hips. Clung to his well-developed thighs. Frayed artfully at the seams. Puckered with just the right suggestion of fullness at his crotch.

Of course, he didn't know there was anything special about the way he wore his pants. The same way he was unaware of the touchable appeal of his perpetually shaggy dark hair. Or the arresting quality of the long-lashed brown eyes, which softened the strong features of his face. He was tall and broad shouldered. As comfortable in the saddle of a horse on his family's ranch as he was in the halls of the hospital where he had been making a name for himself. He was all male. Confident. Strong. In control.

Jarrett's absolute, unquestionable masculinity had struck Ashley the moment they met, when she was seventeen and he not quite two years older. It struck her now, as she ended her silent admiration with a soft "Welcome home, cowboy."

He looked up, surprised.

"Forget I was here?" she teased.

His voice was deep, an appealingly sexy growl. "I figured you'd still be in bed."

Crossing the distance between them with a few quick strides, Ashley flung herself into Jarrett's arms. "Happy wedding day, Dr. McMullen."

Jarrett said nothing, but his arms folded around her, lifting her off the floor and tight against him. The familiar strength of his embrace spread contentment through Ashley. As he settled her back on her feet, his broad hands slid with intimate ease over the oversized T-shirt she had worn to bed. His touch made her shiver.

In his arms was where she belonged. Despite all the odds that had worked against them, this was where she was destined to stay.

Forever.

"Can you believe this is the day?" she whispered. "We're finally getting married."

"I half expected you to be superstitious and meet me at the church."

"After all we've been through, why worry about old wives' tales about the bride not seeing the groom before the ceremony? We're making our own luck this time."

The unshaved stubble of Jarrett's jaw brushed her cheek as he turned his head to kiss her. The touch of his lips was tender, loving. But when he drew away, worry clouded his dark eyes.

Ashley studied the tired lines of his face. "What's wrong? Don't tell me your schedule has changed again. Do you have to pull another shift tonight?"

"No...it's just..." He shoved a hand through dark hair still damp from the shower.

She thought she knew what was bothering him. "You're thinking we should call our families."

"Don't you?"

Her jaw stiffened. "I thought we had already decided. No families."

"Gray will be angry."

Ashley's temper flared at the mention of her older half brother, the man who had raised her and their younger brother following the death of their mother. "I don't care about Gray."

Jarrett gave her a long steady look. "Come on, Ashe. You don't mean that."

She took a deep breath and let it out slowly. "You're right. I do care about Gray. I love him. I just don't want him running my life any longer. If not for Gray, you and I would have been married years and years ago.''

''*We* called off the wedding. Not Gray.''

''Only after he spent months trying to break us up.''

Bitterness flooded Ashley as she recalled the summer after she graduated from high school. She and Jarrett had planned an August wedding in Amarillo, the West Texas town where he had grown up on a ranch and she had moved with her brothers. From the start, Gray had objected to their wedding plans, saying she was far too young. He wanted her to go to college and wait for Jarrett to finish his education and medical training before considering marriage.

Gray's doubts had finally eroded the love Ashley and Jarrett felt for each other. They called off the wedding and went their separate ways.

Until two months ago. When he came home to Amarillo for a visit, and they rediscovered one another.

Ashley slipped her arms around Jarrett. ''I love you. Gray isn't going to come between us this time.''

''Do you really think he would try to stop us now?''

''Eight years may have passed, but Gray still wants to control me.''

Jarrett stepped back, catching her hands in his and studying her with new intensity. ''Gray knows we're back together. I assume you told him you were moving in with me. What's he had to say about it?''

The last thing Ashley wanted to discuss was her

brother, his doubts or his disapproval of the choices she made for her life. She and Gray had had the argument to end all arguments before she came to Dallas to be with Jarrett. Her overprotective big brother thought she was headed for heartbreak. She was bound and determined to prove him wrong.

"Forget Gray," she murmured, and stepped close to lift her lips to Jarrett's once again. "Kiss me instead."

"Ashley…" Jarrett dodged her kiss. "I think we should—"

"Stop thinking," she interjected. "We should stop thinking and make love."

There was no escaping her kiss. Jarrett allowed himself to be pulled along by her hunger for him and the craving he felt for her. He closed his mind to the weariness of the night he had just spent at the hospital, to his worry about the impetuous plans Ashley had made for them. He allowed the dictates of his body and the inclinations of his heart to rule.

Dealing with Ashley was often this way, like trying to change the course of a riptide. The passionate impulsiveness of her nature was what he loved about her, as well as the source of his concern for their future.

Right now, it was easiest to follow the pleasant direction of her mercurial mood. In a matter of moments, Ashley's shirt hit the floor, revealing her golden, smooth skin and the slender curves of her body. She was naked save for the bracelet that had been her mother's. One single golden charm—which

Jarrett had given her just this weekend—glinted as her hands flashed, divesting him of his clothes. Laughing, kissing, teasing, she drew him to his bed, to the rumpled sheets that bore her sweet, delicate scent.

He followed her down. Filled her. Moved with her. In her. Wrapped his mind and his worries and his body in the molten glory that was and always had been Ashley.

How he loved her.

Though he was the one who had been awake going on twenty-four hours, it was Ashley who fell asleep once their passion was spent. Jarrett lay beside her and tried to rest. But questions kept him awake.

He did not welcome his doubts. He wanted to believe, as Ashley did, that fate had brought them back together, that marriage was the goal for which they had been preparing all this time. He loved her. There were no doubts there. But marriage? Were they once again rushing headlong into commitment?

Giving up on sleep, he eased out of bed, pulled on his jeans and found his way to the worn leather recliner in the corner of the living room. This chair, a castoff of his father's, had seen him through the difficult years of medical school and internship. Many times he had arrived home and collapsed here, never making it to bed.

Jarrett was the first to admit he had not been prepared for the gut-chewing intensity of his medical training. There was a time when he would have done anything rather than admit Ashley's brother Gray was right, but the man had been correct in worrying how a young marriage would be affected by the rigors of his studies. Jarrett wasn't sure he and Ashley would have made it.

More hard work lay ahead of him. Jarrett had decided to specialize in plastic surgery; he faced more training, more eighteen-hour shifts and long, sleepless nights. He had seen marriages buckle under the strain these past few years. Could Ashley handle the pressure?

She had grown from a headstrong, impulsive girl into a headstrong, impulsive woman. She was beautiful. Exciting. But ruled by emotion, by the vagaries of her quick mind and her many interests. What made her fascinating could also infuriate.

Her arrival at his apartment this past weekend illustrated his concerns. He thought she was coming for a visit, as she had done most every weekend since their romance had rekindled. Instead, she had given up her job and apartment in Amarillo. Her furniture was stored, and most of her clothes were packed in the suitcases stacked in the corner of the bedroom. She blew in like a tornado. In the dizzy, intoxicating whirl Ashley spun so skillfully, they had made plans for today's elopement.

At the hospital, away from her, Jarrett reconsidered those plans. He reconsidered them now.

With a sigh, he laid his head against upholstery softened by age and use.

Ashley spoke from the doorway. ''What's wrong?''

She had slipped back into her sleep shirt, and looked very young and very vulnerable standing there. Jarrett couldn't find the right words to frame his doubts.

The green-gold splendor of her eyes dimmed as she advanced into the room and knelt beside his chair. "Tell me."

Jarrett cleared his throat. "Aren't you afraid we've moved a little too fast?"

Bright spots of color appeared in her cheeks. "Fast? My God, for years—"

"Years apart," he interrupted. "We both moved on."

"But when I saw you when you came home…when we looked at one another…" She stood up abruptly, unsteady on her feet. "You don't want to marry me."

The hurt in her expression twisted his insides. He stood and faced her. "That's not what I said."

"But you're backing off."

"I'm trying to think rationally. Logically."

"You're saying you don't love me."

"No." His denial was swift and sure. "This isn't about love. It's about going off in a fever to get married without our friends and our families."

"I thought we only needed each other."

He took her hands again. "We need to catch our breaths."

Her lovely face went still and cold as she pulled away from him. "You sound like Gray. With him, it's always slow down, think it through, look before you leap—''

"None of those things are necessarily bad advice."

"Last time we decided to think it through, we fell apart."

"That won't happen this time." Jarrett stepped close to her again. "I love you, Ashley. But I also want us to do this the right way. I know the best way for both of us."

Anger momentarily warmed her cool gaze. "What's the best way? You mean *your* way, don't you?"

He blew out an impatient breath. "I wish you would try to see my point of view. I don't want you to go back to Amarillo. I want you to stay here in Dallas. Maybe go back to school. Find a job you really want. I want us to spend every possible moment together. But let me get through this last year of my residency before we get married. Then we'll have the biggest, most beautiful wedding you've ever imagined. We'll start our married life together on the right note."

Her fingers squeezed his. "I don't want a big wedding. I want you. Now."

"Why is that so important? Why the rush?"

"I don't want us to let what we have slip away again."

"It won't."

"You can't guarantee that."

Jarrett gave an impatient sigh. "Come on, Ashe,

can't you see the wisdom of waiting? There's no reason to sneak off like two kids. This next year is going to be hell for me. It's just sensible to wait, to not be so impulsive.''

His cautionary tone set off a drumbeat inside Ashley.

Be sensible.

Be reasonable.

Be careful.

These were the warnings she had heard from most everyone for years. From Gray. From his wife, Kathryn, who used to be her ally. From her younger brother, Rick, who once believed she could do no wrong. From friends. And teachers. And bosses.

They had all wanted her to stay in college, even though she hadn't a clue as to what she wanted to study. They wanted her to keep each of the dead-end, boring jobs that came her way. They wanted her to meet some nice, sedate man. They wanted her to be wary of hooking up with Jarrett once more. They wanted her to hold back, rein in her feelings, live a little slower.

Be anything but yourself, Ashley.

Once upon a time, Jarrett had convinced her she shouldn't listen to those warnings, that she should believe in herself and listen to her heart. When they reconnected, she thought he could make her feel that way again. She thought he accepted her for who and what she was. But now here he was—hitting the brakes, casting doubt on what she knew was true, that they belonged together. To hell with waiting.

They'd waited far too long. To hell with being sensible. Why not follow the heat of their dreams? Waiting had brought them nothing once before. Why chance it again?

"I can't believe you want to do this to us," she whispered, heartbreak clogging her throat.

Jarrett's brow furrowed. "Ashley, can't you hear what I'm saying? I want to postpone the wedding, not cancel it. I want us to be smart this time."

"And pledging ourselves to each other isn't smart?" Oh, that hurt. Hurt so badly.

"Just think about it," Jarrett urged. "Just calm down. You'll see it's for the best that we wait."

He sounded like her brother. Like everyone who ever wanted to make her decisions for her. Ashley backed away, ice forming in the blood so recently heated by Jarrett's lovemaking. Something clicked shut in her brain.

By God, this was it. This was the end of being questioned and held back, of being told how to think and act and feel.

She turned on her heel and headed for the bedroom. Jarrett followed, still pleading his case, but she closed him out, intent on what she had to do. Thankfully, most of her clothes were still packed; she wouldn't have to waste any time. She found jeans and a T-shirt, shoes and socks. Only when she went to the bathroom and tossed cosmetics in a bag did Jarrett seem to realize she was leaving.

"That's enough," he said, his voice deep and

forceful as he filled the doorway. "You're not going anywhere."

Her answer was to push past him and toss the makeup bag into an open suitcase. She was zipping the case shut when Jarrett took hold of her arm. She shook him off, but his fingers closed around her forearm again. She looked up at him. "What are you going to do? Hold me here by brute force?"

Jarrett, who would sooner shoot himself than harm a woman, backed away. Anger flushed his face crimson. "Damn it, Ashe, why do you want to act like such a damn fool?"

She slung the strap of her purse over her shoulder. "You've made me a fool. A fool for believing in you."

"You're acting as irrational and bullheaded as Gray always accuses you of being."

"The two of you can get together and gloat over always being so right about me." With a suitcase clutched in one hand and the other dragging behind her, she marched toward the door.

She paused for only a moment, to look up at her wedding dress. Bought years ago. Treasured. Saved. Dreamed over. She hesitated. Then left it hanging.

Jarrett followed her out the door into the warmth of the spring day. Her aging blue Honda was parked only a short distance away, near his red pickup. He stood, bare chested and seething, on the sidewalk outside his apartment and watched her throw her suitcases in the trunk.

"All right," he said when she fumbled with the

keys in the door. "You've made your point. Now come back in and let's talk this out."

"No, thank you," she replied. "You've made your point, too. I'm leaving."

"And in an hour you'll be back. Save us both the drama, would you, please?"

The urge to slap him was so strong she trembled. Instead, she turned the keys in the lock and got in the car. Jarrett leaped forward and grabbed the edge of the door before she could pull it shut.

"Let go," she said, feeling oddly calm.

"Where are you going?"

She slammed the door on his concern. On her dreams.

She drove away.

Jarrett stood in the April sunshine. Furious with her. With himself. He watched her leave, then stalked back inside and waited for the phone to ring. Waited for her to say he was right and she was sorry.

He waited for a phone call that never came.

Chapter One

Tired from his flight, irritated by a delay with his luggage, Jarrett emerged from the airport terminal in Vancouver, British Columbia, with a sigh of relief. He needed a taxi, a quick trip to his hotel and a good night's sleep before his medical conference started tomorrow.

He was moving toward a waiting cab when he saw her.

Petite. Blond. A purple velvet hat with a funky red flower pulled low over her forehead. She was wearing a dark cape. Very dramatic. Very...*Ashley.*

His heart knocked hard against his ribs. So loud he wasn't sure if he forced her name past his lips or not. Somehow, he crossed the expanse of concrete that separated them. She turned.

She wasn't Ashley.

The woman, the *stranger,* spoke in heavily accented English, "Yes? Can I help you?"

Jarrett swallowed his disappointment. "I'm sorry, miss. I thought you were someone else."

Maybe something in his expression roused the woman's sympathy, for her smile was kind. *"Pardon, monsieur,"* she murmured.

"No, excuse me," Jarrett replied, then backed away.

The entire cab ride to the hotel passed before his pulse stopped hammering. Even then, he kept seeing the woman standing there, kept replaying the moment when she turned. If only she had been Ashley.

After leaving him in Dallas three years ago, Ashley had gone to California. For almost a month, no one knew where she was. She finally got in touch with her family, though she refused to tell them anything more than she was fine. Once he got over his relief, he had been furious. Too angry to think of following her, even if she had been willing to reveal her location.

In the months that followed, her contact with her family had been spotty. They knew she had lived for five months in an apartment complex near Encino. She had worked for a temporary agency. One day, she packed up and left. There was evidence she had sold her car. The dealer who bought it thought a man had been with her. That man was the end of the trail. And the beginning of a nightmare for everyone who cared about Ashley.

Jarrett settled into his hotel, bone tired but unable to contemplate sleep. He could go along for days, a week even, with only a fleeting thought of Ashley. His life was busy with the plastic-surgery practice he had just joined, friends, commitments. He dated other women, had given some thought to marriage last year.

And then there were days when Ashley was on his mind constantly. Days like today, when he saw someone with the look of her and his hopes rose and crashed.

Odds were slim to none he would just happen to see Ashley. But he never stopped studying people. He looked hardest at women with long, blond hair. Particularly if they were small and slender. Or if they walked with an easy, natural grace. Or if they tilted their heads to the side while they studied a magazine or a shop window's display. There were no guarantees that Ashley looked as she once had, but he couldn't stop searching.

Occasionally, Jarrett thought he heard Ashley's voice. Or her laughter. Full and throaty. As welcome as a gusher in an oil field gone dry.

But Ashley was never there.

For a long time, he didn't tell anyone how often he looked for her, but he had found companionship in his fruitless search in Ashley's family. Her brother Gray and his wife, Kathryn, admitted how they scanned the crowds on televised events, hoping, praying, for a glimpse of her. Her younger brother, Rick, who had grown into a young man of eighteen since Ashley disappeared, had focused his hopes on the true-crime television programs that profiled missing persons. Ashley's photograph had been shown twice. No calls. No leads. Nothing.

Jarrett wondered if the people Ashley had left behind would spend the rest of their lives searching the faces of strangers and waiting for evidence she was still alive.

His head told him she must be dead. As upset as Ashley had been with him when she left, he couldn't believe she would cause this much grief by disappearing on purpose without one word. Ashley had been headstrong, impulsive and dramatic. But never cruel. Never uncaring. Surely she wouldn't torture her family this way, no matter how angry or confused she might have been when she left.

On the other hand, Jarrett thought he would know, instinctively, if Ashley was really gone. He wasn't a strong believer in mysticism or psychic connections. But surely his heart would feel her absence from this world. His heart was certain she was alive somewhere.

Why did he let her drive away?

He always cycled back to that question. He should have made her stay with him. Held her in the apartment by force, if necessary. Made her listen to him. Made her understand he loved her, that they would be married.

Logically, he knew he couldn't have known Ashley was going to disappear. But he also felt he should have known she had reached some point of no return. Why hadn't he seen how very upset she had been?

When these questions started, the guilt was never far behind. Every time he thought of Ashley, guilt rolled over him like a river. Wide and deep. Sometimes, he was afraid he would drown in it.

That emotion nagged at him now, in this strange hotel room. He was edgy, reliving old hurts and questionable decisions. He couldn't put Ashley out of his mind. It was as if he could feel her. Most likely, this was fallout from the woman at the airport who had looked like her. He couldn't shake his anxiety.

As the hours wore on, he finally flipped on the television and drifted in and out of an uneasy sleep. He jolted awake again and again, thinking he heard Ashley call his name.

The next morning, he was dressing for the start of the medical conference when a local news program flashed the photograph of a young woman on the television screen.

Hair the color of the lightest honey.

Big eyes, gold, as well.

Her beautiful features set in sad lines.

Jarrett's knees went weak. He sank to the end of the bed, staring at the screen, at the woman. Vaguely, he heard the news anchor say she had been found in a small British Columbia town northeast of Vancouver. She had been disoriented and alone, apparently the victim of a mugging, with no identifying papers or belongings, unable to recall where she came from or where she was going. She didn't even know her name.

But Jarrett did.

Ashley.

The hospital nurses called her Anne. It was a simple, compact name, and it had some basis in fact. Several days ago, when she was finally able to stay awake for more than a few moments at a time, a nurse had given her a bracelet that had been found in the pocket of her jeans. Whatever other jewelry she might have worn—like a wedding ring—had vanished with the rest of her possessions. This bracelet was the only clue to her identity thus far. An ornate *A* was inscribed on the bracelet's one gold charm. Just an *A*.

For Anne.

Or Amy. Amelia. Agnes.

The possibilities marched through her head as she twisted the bracelet around and around on her wrist. None of those names felt right. For all intents and purposes, she had no name. Even the face that looked back at her in the mirror was that of a stranger.

It had become clear that she remembered the rudiments of civilized living. She could talk, walk, feed and bathe herself. Last night while watching a program on television, she had laughed and told a nurse it was one of her favorites. Yet she couldn't name the characters or anything about the show's background. The limitations of that particular memory reassured her; she didn't know how she would feel if she could remember fiction better than the facts of her own life.

She turned from the mirror on the wall and crossed to the hospital room's window. In contrast to her fog-shrouded mind, the September day was crystal clear. She could see a blue lake in the distance, glimmering in the afternoon sun. Mountains rose to snowcapped peaks, towering over the valley. This town was a beautiful place. Peaceful. If the people who worked in the hospital were any indication, it was a nice town in which to live.

Soon she would have to think about where she was going to go. She was physically sound. The room and bed she occupied and the food she ate belonged to someone in genuine need. Maybe the town outside her window was a place where she could find a job, settle down, raise a family.

Those very thoughts mocked her. How could she have a family when she didn't know who she was? Pressing a hand to her stomach, she fought a rising tide of panic.

A knock sounded on the half-opened door of her room. She turned to find Dr. Tiernan, his usual kind, sweet smile in place. The stout, older man was a psychiatrist, called in on her case when tests showed there was no physical reason, no clearcut neurological cause for her inability to regain her memory. She had been hit on the head, or bumped her head in a fall, but the injury was relatively minor, like the exposure, exhaustion, some minor cuts, bruises and twisted ankle she was also suffering from. Whatever trauma had erased her memory appeared mental, not physical.

"How are you this afternoon?" the doctor asked as the door swung shut behind him.

She smiled in return. Of all the doctors, nurses and police officers who had paraded through her life this past week, she felt most comfortable with this man. "I'm a little stir-crazy," she told him, then laughed. "But I guess that's to be expected since I'm some kind of lunatic."

Wagging a finger in disapproval, Dr. Tiernan joined her beside the window. "How many times do I have to tell you? You're not crazy."

"I just want to remember something. Someone. Myself."

"We talked about not pushing so hard."

"How am I supposed to do that?" To her chagrin, her voice broke on the last word.

Dr. Tiernan's touch on her arm was gentle, his tone calm and soothing. "You know you have to try to relax. Your memory won't come back by force."

She took a deep breath. Dr. Tiernan had shown her that if she could relax, even a little bit, these choking moments of panic would recede. Last night, when she had managed to lose herself in that television program, a memory, however insignificant, had surfaced.

The doctor rested one shoulder against the wall beside the window and asked her about that memory. "The nurse noted on your chart that you said that program was your favorite. How did you know that?"

"The words just popped out."

"You don't remember watching the program with anyone? Your family, maybe?"

She shook her head. "That's what is so weird about it. It's like a free-floating memory. Not attached to anything at all."

"But it's a beginning. That's how it could all come back, little by little."

She tugged at the belt of her thin, hospital-issue robe. "It could take me the rest of my life to remember the first part of my life."

"I doubt that. If we could get you home, among familiar people and places…"

She gave the doctor a sharp look. "How's that supposed to happen when I can't remember where I'm from? When no one's come forward…"

The abrupt way Dr. Tiernan straightened his shoulders spoke volumes.

"What is it? Has someone come for me?" Both hopeful and terrified by the possibility, she glanced toward the closed door. "Is there someone here?"

Dr. Tiernan once again took hold of her arm. "Just a minute now. Hang on."

"But if there's someone who can identify me—"

"We think there is," the doctor said. "Your photograph ran on a Vancouver television station this morning. Someone thought he recognized you. The police have been checking him and his story out all day, and it looks good. But we want to be careful, of course.''

''Careful?'' The word caught in her throat. ''My God, what's there to lose?''

He kept his voice calm and controlled. ''My dear, you were found in the middle of the night, wandering down a street. Lost and confused. With no ID, no clue as to who you are. You've obviously been through a terrible experience. We don't want to place you back in the hands of someone who might have caused that trauma.''

That made sense. Even to someone as befuddled as her. She drew in another calming breath and counted to ten.

''We want you to meet this man.''

''Now?'' Instinctively, she ran a hand through her hair and turned to the mirror.

Dr. Tiernan chuckled. ''You certainly haven't forgotten the usual feminine responses.''

Though she knew he was only trying to put her at ease, she couldn't hide her impatience. ''Please, Doctor—''

''All right.'' He strode to the door and gave her one last, reassuring smile before pulling it open.

She glimpsed a police officer she recognized, but no one else. In a nervous gesture she realized was becoming a habit, she twisted the charm on her bracelet.

A man stepped in the door. Tall and broad shouldered. Dark hair. Steady, dark eyes. His name came floating up from somewhere in the depths of her shattered mind. "Jarrett."

A smile broke across his tense features. As he crossed the room toward her, she could see tears in his eyes. "Ashley, my God. It's you. Really you. And you know me."

Her gaze locked on the face of this stranger, she repeated the name he called her. "Ashley. Is that my name?"

He stopped before reaching her, his smile fading. "Ashley Elizabeth Grant."

She felt no rush of recognition. She felt…nothing.

Dr. Tiernan stepped up to the stranger's side. "You called this man by name."

"But I don't know why." She began to tremble. "I don't know him. Why don't I know?"

"Ashley…" The stranger closed the remaining distance between them in one step. His arms went around her.

She didn't resist his embrace, but she couldn't return it, either, not until she had some answers. "Who are you?" she whispered.

He drew away, though his hands remained on her shoulders, his gaze steady on hers. "Ashley. What's happened to you? Where have you been?"

"Don't you know?"

Dr. Tiernan spoke up again. "Dr. McMullen, as I told you—"

"Doctor?" she repeated, puzzled, looking from Tiernan and back to the stranger. "You're a doctor, too?"

''Dr. Jarrett McMullen,'' the stranger clarified.

''And how do I know you? Was I in some kind of hospital?''

''Of course not. Ashley, you know who I am.'' His hands framed her face. ''You called me by name when I walked in here. We've known each other for over ten years. We were going to be married.''

''We were?''

He reached down and lifted her arm. His long fingers circled the chunky gold bracelet. ''I gave you this. That last weekend in Dallas. Don't you remember?''

She stared long and hard at the bracelet. *A* for Ashley. She looked at Jarrett McMullen. ''You gave me the bracelet?''

He shook his head. ''Just the charm. The bracelet was your mother's.''

''My mother?'' She closed her eyes, and there was the briefest flash of memory. A laughing woman, a child in her arms. Music as they danced in a sun-filled room.

''My mother,'' she said again. ''Where is she?''

''You remember her?'' Dr. Tiernan asked, his voice soft.

''I…'' Images flickered through her brain. Outlines. Nothing concrete. ''I don't know.'' She lifted her gaze to the stranger named Jarrett. ''Where is my mother?''

Muscles worked in his throat as he swallowed. ''Ashe…don't you remember? Your mother is…she's gone. She died before I ever met you. You were only eleven. It was before you moved to Amarillo. With Gray and Rick.''

A dull ache had started in her temples. ''Amarillo? Gray and Rick? But who——?''

''Dr. McMullen,'' Tiernan interrupted. ''Please. Don't bombard her with information.''

''But surely she remembers her brothers. Her family.''

She pressed a hand to her stomach. ''I don't.''

Silence fell in the room. Jarrett McMullen studied her with the perplexed frown she had grown used to seeing on people's faces. Only it was different, of course, because he believed he knew her.

She felt compelled to say something to him. ''I'm sorry. Maybe I'm not who you think I am.''

He shook his head, then reached for his wallet. From a side pocket came a photograph. Bent at the corners. Creased along one edge, as if it had been caught in the fold of the wallet. The face in the picture was younger than the one she had been studying in the mirror just a short while ago. But unmistakably her face.

''This was made about four years ago.'' Jarrett flipped it over. In faded black ink, the inscription on the back read For Jarrett. Love, Ashley.

Before she could respond, the police officer, who had stepped into the room, cleared his throat. ''There's more proof, Miss Grant.''

She frowned at the still unfamiliar name he called her. ''What proof?''

The officer explained that when Jarrett had contacted the authorities this morning, they had gotten in touch with the police in California, where a missing-person's report had been on file with her picture. Everything checked out. Jarrett had even been able to describe the bracelet she now wore.

"And you called him by name," the officer said. "When he walked in here, he was supposed to be making sure you were the right person. But you recognized him."

"But I don't know why. I don't know him." Her voice rose as her heart began to pound.

Dr. Tiernan reached for her hand before the panic could overtake her. "Relax now. Take a deep breath. This is what you wanted—to know your name, where you're from and where you've been. We're sure this is the truth, *Ashley*." He smiled as he said the name that was still so new to her. "We wouldn't push this if we weren't certain."

He was right. She trusted him, as she had from the very beginning. She gripped his hand and stared at Jarrett McMullen. He said he had known her for over ten years, that they were going to be married. If that was true, then some of her deepest, most troubling worries were over. He might be a stranger except for his name, but he didn't look like someone who would walk away from his responsibilities. He was well dressed and clearly successful, a doctor. And he was here. He had walked in and taken her in his arms. Surely they must love one another. And that would make everything all right.

Jarrett's eyes were kind as he spoke to her again.

"I'm going to look after you, Ashley. I'm going to make sure you're never lost or hurt again."

The reassurance in his gaze and his voice drained some of the fear and tension from her.

"Your family will be here as soon as I can reach them," he added. "We'll take you home."

"Where is that?"

"They live in Amarillo, Texas, where you and I met. I'm still in Dallas."

"Still?" she repeated, confused.

"I stayed in Dallas after I finished my medical training," he explained.

She frowned, realizing there were pieces of this puzzle that didn't add up. "Why was there a missing-person's report on me in California if I lived in Texas?"

"You had moved to California."

"How long have I been gone?"

An uneasy glance traveled among the three men.

"What is it?" she asked. "Why do you all look so funny?"

Jarrett stepped forward again. "You've been gone for a long time, Ashley. Three years."

Several moments passed while she tried to absorb his words. "It's been three years since you've seen me?"

"Three years since anyone has heard from you."

She pressed a hand to her stomach, her heart sinking. "If I haven't seen you in three years..." She swallowed, unable to go any further.

"What?" he demanded. "What's wrong?"

Somehow, she found her voice again and forced herself to meet his gaze. "If I haven't seen you for three years, then you can't be the father of this baby."

His face went pale. "Baby?"

Very softly, Dr. Tiernan explained, "There's one thing we didn't tell you, Dr. McMullen. Ashley is around three months pregnant."

The shock and confusion on Jarrett McMullen's face mirrored Ashley's own swirling emotions. Since he wasn't this baby's father, who was? Why had the man left her? Where was he now?

Without a name or a face to put with the father, how was she ever going to feel any connection to the child, the stranger growing in her womb?

Not since the day she woke up here in the hospital and realized her predicament had she dissolved into tears. Now she buried her face in her hands and fought back a sob. Someone reached out to her, pulled her close.

Low against her ear, Jarrett McMullen said, "It's okay, Ashley."

For a moment, she tried to resist, instinctively wanting to hide the weakness of her tears.

He seemed to know she didn't want to break down in front of them all. Quietly, he asked if Dr. Tiernan and the officer could give them a few minutes. When they were gone, his arms tightened around her once again. His chest was broad, solid beneath her cheek.

"Cry it out," he told her. "It's just me, Ashley. You've cried in front of me before."

"Have I?"

"Get the crying over with. Then it's going to be okay. I promise you it's all going to be okay."

"But how?" she choked out. "I don't know myself. I don't know the father of this child. How can it be okay?"

"Because I'm here now. I'm here and you're safe. You and your baby are safe."

She knew, in a sudden flash of knowledge, that she had relied on the confidence in his voice and the strength in his arms before today.

She allowed herself to lean on this man. She cried while Jarrett held her tight.

Chapter Two

"When can we get Ashley out of here?"

The question from Ashley's brother was as direct as Jarrett would have expected from such a straight shooter. Gray and his wife, Kathryn, had arrived at this small Canadian hospital less than eighteen hours after Jarrett called them with the news that Ashley had been found.

The family reunion was somewhat strained, given that Ashley couldn't have picked her brother and sister-in-law out of a police lineup. They were complete strangers to her. When that became clear, Kathryn, and then Ashley, fell apart. Gray Nolan remained strong. After a couple of hours of playing comforter to the women of his family, Gray excused himself, ostensibly to talk with Dr. Tiernan. When a half hour passed without Gray returning to Ashley's room, Jarrett found him sitting in the visitors' lounge, his face buried in his hands, bawling like a baby.

But that was over now. A man who had spent his entire adult life making decisions for his family, Gray was ready for the next step. "I want to get Ashley home. Right away. I don't want her story picked up by every tabloid in the world."

"As far as I know, the police department and hospital simply released statements that she had been identified by her family."

"Let's hope it stays that simple. Do you see any reason why we can't start for home tonight?"

"Physically, she seems fine. As far as her mental state, I doubt anyone would disagree with the benefits of taking her back to a place that's familiar, around people who love her. I'd say getting her home will be a simple matter of clearing some final details with the authorities."

Gray pushed himself to his feet, his hands fisting at his sides. "I just wish someone had found the man who let this happen to her."

Jarrett agreed. "Last night, even after she fell asleep, I couldn't leave her and go to my hotel. I kept thinking, what if some creep is out there, waiting for a chance to get at her again?"

"How could someone abandon her? Only a low-life scum would abandon a pregnant woman."

Many possibilities had presented themselves to Jarrett. Hesitantly, he offered them to Gray. "What if no one abandoned her? The guy might not even know she's having a baby.''

''Even so, there's obviously a man in her life. Why hasn't he come forward? From what the authorities have told us, Ashley's face has been featured all over the news in this area. Whoever the father of that baby is should have moved heaven and earth to get to her.''

''We could hire a private investigator, like you did a couple of years ago.''

''He came up with zilch.''

''But now he could try to retrace Ashley's steps, go farther up into Canada.''

''Maybe.'' Gray didn't appear too enthused.

Jarrett thought he understood why. He suspected Gray was afraid to find out the whole truth. Some memories might just as well be buried. What if Ashley had been raped? Held somewhere by some psycho?

The very idea made his stomach churn. If Ashley had endured the unthinkable, part of the blame belonged to him. One glance at her brother's face showed Gray was suffering through much the same self-torture.

Gray raked his hand through dark hair liberally threaded with gray. He looked tired, the lines in his face chronicling each of his forty-three years. For the first time, Jarrett saw clear evidence of what the worry and fear over Ashley had done to her brother. Jarrett had never been close to this man. In fact, they had argued more than they had agreed. After Ashley's disappearance, Gray had made no secret of blaming Jarrett. But Jarrett wasn't about to dwell on that now.

"She's going to be all right." Jarrett gave Gray's shoulder a brief squeeze of reassurance. "No matter what's happened to her, she's going to be fine."

"I don't know if I can ever let her out of my sight again."

Jarrett laughed. "Once upon a time, those kind of words would have had Ashley mad as a cornered rattlesnake."

A line appeared between Gray's eyebrows. "She seems so different. So quiet."

"You can't expect her not to have changed."

Gray paused for a moment, his gaze searching Jarrett's face. "How are you feeling about all this?"

"Ashley being found?"

"I'm talking about the baby, about Ashley carrying some stranger's child. How does that make you feel?"

In the long hours Jarrett had spent watching Ashley sleep last night, he had shied away from that question again and again. Leave it to Gray to bring it right out in the open.

"I'm not sure," Jarrett said, finally. "Right now, I'm just glad we've found her. That she's alive."

"I know." Gray sighed and shook his head. "I wish to hell this were the end of her troubles."

"It's the end of most of them."

"But what about this baby?" Gray asked.

"The doctors say she's healthy, that the baby is,

too, as far as they can tell. They've done a sonogram. Ashley's been tested for disease. She's fine.''

''Can any of their tests tell her how to feel about a child whose father she can't remember?''

''She's going to need her family to help her get through this.''

Silent for a moment, Gray let out a deep breath. ''You're right.''

Before Gray could reply, his wife came across the lounge, frowning. ''What are the two of you doing in here? I'd think you'd want to be with Ashley.''

''I needed some time to collect myself,'' Gray told her. ''I didn't want her to see me fall apart.''

An understanding smile touched Kathryn's lips as she slipped an arm around her husband's waist. ''It's been quite a day, hasn't it?''

At forty-one, Kathryn Seeger Nolan was a sleek and lovely woman. Aside from a short and sophisticated style for her ebony hair, she hadn't changed much from the first time Jarrett had met her, when he was just a kid. His older sister, Paige, and Kathryn had been friends in college, and it was during her visits to Amarillo that Kathryn had decided to make the city her home upon graduation. She still owned the wedding boutique where Ashley had gone to buy a gown when she and Jarrett were planning to marry. Their wedding-that-never-was brought Kathryn and Gray together. Only Ashley's disappearance had marred the life they shared with their two young daughters.

Jarrett couldn't help wondering how things would

have turned out if he and Ashley had gone through with their plans the first time they decided to marry. She sure as hell wouldn't be here. Her memory wouldn't be scattered. She wouldn't be pregnant by another man.

His thoughts firmly on what-might-have-been's, Jarrett wasn't aware that anyone had spoken to him until he felt a touch on his arm. He looked up.

Kathryn regarded him with a troubled expression. "Are you okay?"

Nodding, he chased the stormy thoughts from his head. "What's up?"

"Ashley is asking for you."

"Is she all right?"

"I think she just feels safer with you around," Kathryn replied. "You are the only one of us she's recognized."

"She knew my name," Jarrett corrected her. "She doesn't know me."

"But that gives you a leg up on any of us." Gray looked none too pleased by that state of affairs. "I'm just glad we brought pictures to show her we're her family. Otherwise, she might not believe us."

Jarrett knew the sooner they took Ashley home, the sooner this entire family would begin to heal. "Why don't I go back and stay with her while the two of you see if we can get her out of here to-night?"

Gray and Kathryn went in search of Dr. Tiernan while Jarrett hurried back to Ashley's room. Having changed from her hospital garb to some jeans and a sweater Kathryn had brought, she appeared much as she had the night she left him in Dallas. Thinner, maybe. But even without makeup, with her blond hair caught back in a ponytail, she was still the amber-eyed beauty who had captured his heart so long ago.

"You're looking like yourself," Jarrett said, pausing in the doorway. Too late he realized his words sounded cruel, since she didn't have a clue as to how she should look. He started a fumbling apology.

Ashley rose from her chair. "Please don't edit everything you say to me. Just be natural and normal."

"That's a tall order, considering the situation."

"But I want everyone to treat me the way they would if this hadn't happened." Her expression grew pensive. "Gray doesn't know what to say to me."

"That's not really too far off the mark from normal." Last night, Jarrett had done his best to explain Ashley's relationship with her family, hoping the information would help her adjust or would prompt a memory.

Sighing, Ashley turned to gaze out the window.

Jarrett crossed the room and perched beside her on the broad windowsill. "Tell me what you're thinking, Ashe."

"I wish I could remember something about Gray and Kathryn."

"You will."

"They obviously care about me. Maybe I should be comforted, but instead I'm all out of sorts. I don't know how to react to them."

Jarrett took her hand. "You loved them. Gray drove you crazy sometimes, and the two of you were never great at communicating, but you loved him a lot."

"That's what Kathryn said."

"You can trust Kathryn. She's never steered any of us wrong. She was a good mediator those times when you and Gray clashed."

"She acts like she knows me very well. But still..." Ashley glanced at the family photographs spread across her bed. There were photos of their family home, of her younger brother, of her nieces, of her closest friends, of holidays and special events, of her and Jarrett. None of the snapshots roused any memories.

Her distress was clear as she gazed at those pictures.

"It may feel different when you see Rick," Jarrett suggested, thinking of her younger brother. "You and he were really close."

Ashley's doubtful expression was unchanged.

"Gray and Kathryn have gone to see if there's any reason why you can't go home just as soon as possible."

Her eyes widened, wary instead of pleased.

"Don't you want to go home?"

"I don't remember home."

He squeezed the fingers of the hand he still held. "I think you stand your best chance of remembering everything there."

"Dr. Tiernan says there are no guarantees I'll ever remember."

"He was just being cautious. We doctors don't like to make absolute promises. But the averages are on your side. Once you're safely at home, memories will probably start coming back. Maybe little by little. Maybe all at once. You could wake up and remember it all."

Her other hand fluttered to rest on her stomach. He wondered if she was thinking as he and Gray had, that there were some memories she might not want to recall.

"We'll deal with everything, Ashe."

"*We* will?"

"All of us. Your friends and family."

She tugged her hand free of his. "You live in Dallas."

"That's right."

"But I'll be in Amarillo, with Gray and Kathryn and their daughters."

"Yes, but—"

"So you won't be dealing with anything." An accusatory note slipped into her voice. "When I asked, Kathryn told me all about us. She told me the truth. You lied yesterday when you said we were engaged."

Jarrett frowned. "That's not true. Though our engagement might not have been official, we were going to be married."

"But I left you. Kathryn said we argued and I left."

"An argument doesn't mean we wouldn't have found our way back together."

"Kathryn says we almost married twice. Both times we—or you—got cold feet."

"The last time, before you left, all we disagreed about was the timing."

"Why didn't you explain it all to me yesterday?"

"I thought you had enough to handle."

"But the way you acted yesterday...you let me believe...I thought..." Red suffused her pale cheeks.

"You thought we were still together," Jarrett completed for her.

Her color deepened. "I knew that couldn't be true. We've been apart three years. Obviously, I..." Again, her hand touched her stomach. "I've obviously formed another attachment. But then, when you stayed with me all night, I thought...I wondered..." She broke off in utter confusion.

"I care about you," Jarrett insisted.

She turned her gaze toward the window again. "Kathryn says all of you knew I was in California for a while. Did you contact me there?"

There was nothing Jarrett could tell her but the truth. "No, I didn't. I was angry with you for running away. I decided to let well enough alone."

"Well enough." Repeating those words, Ashley once again folded her arms across her middle, protectively, as if shielding the child she carried.

Pain twisted inside Jarrett and roughened his voice. "I wish I could go back, Ashe. If I could do it over, I never would have let you drive away from me. Failing that, I certainly would have gone to California and brought you home."

She looked at him then, with a flash of the Ashley he knew so well in her golden gaze. "Do you think I would have just come home. Just because you came for me?"

That gave him pause. He realized he had spent the past few years thinking that if he had found her, she would have fallen into his arms again. And yet...why not? Despite the way she ran away from him, hadn't they loved one another? Hadn't they always?

Even when they were just kids, after they called off their wedding the first time, they had continued to circle each other like cats in heat. For years, he had avoided the holiday get-togethers that forced them together. Not because he didn't want to see Ashley. But because he wanted to see her too much. Even when he was dating someone else. And especially when she was seeing someone.

God, how he had hated those visits home to Amarillo when he accidentally ran into her with another guy. The jealousy had torn him apart. He had been unable to stop thinking of another man's lips on hers, another man's hands on her body.

He had tried to rationalize his feelings. He told himself his possessiveness stemmed from his being Ashley's first lover, when she was just eighteen and they were planning their wedding. After they broke up, he had kept his feelings in check for years. Until that holiday he came home and ran into her in an Amarillo bar, a hangout for their old friends. She had been with a group of girlfriends, looking so gorgeous, so…Ashley.

The memory of that dizzy, crazy week heated Jarrett's blood even now. A glance at Ashley made him wonder if she might be able to remember that time, as well. Surely she would recall the way they had flirted that first night they ran into each other. How they had ended up back at her apartment. Just to talk, she had said. Just to talk, he had agreed. But they wound up in bed, acting on the love that had been simmering beneath the surface for so many years, rekindling a passion that had never died.

He spent every night of that vacation with her. And most of his days. She called in sick to the real-estate office where she was a receptionist. They rediscovered how the rhythm of their bodies could match the union of their hearts. Those days and nights, she turned to him again and again. Insatiable. Tender. Loving.

If he reminded Ashley of those sweet, intimate moments, would he reach past the fog that shrouded her memories? Or would he cause her even more pain? Certainly, the memories brought him as much agony as pleasure. For he couldn't help wondering about what might have been.

While he sorted through the memories, trying to decide what to share with her, Ashley studied him, her head cocked to one side. "You feel guilty about me."

The observation came fron the old Ashley, the one from whom he could never hide his emotions. "We all feel guilty, Ashe. We all wish we had brought you home.''

Her chin tilted up. ''Do you really think you could have?''

Again, the challenge in this remark held the spirit of the old Ashley, as well. Jarrett grinned. ''Not only are you looking like yourself—you sound like yourself, too.''

''I just wish I knew what 'myself' means.''

''It'll come. It's already coming.'' Once again, he took her hand.

Ashley resisted the urge to pull away. Jarrett McMullen touched her a lot. Her hand. Her face. Her hair. He reached out to her often, with easy familiarity. Last night, when she awakened to find him dozing beside her bed, one of his hands had been resting lightly on her arm, as if he feared she would be wrenched away from him again. The thought that he was nearby, watching over her, was so comforting she had slept through the rest of the night, something she hadn't done since the worst of her exhaustion dissipated after her first few days in the hospital.

This morning, while she waited for her brother and Kathryn to arrive, Ashley had allowed herself to hope Jarrett would be her salvation. She daydreamed that he might love her in spite of her wounded mind. In spite of the stranger's baby growing inside her.

But he wasn't her white knight. He wasn't this child's father.

She told herself it didn't matter. Clearly, she had a family who loved her. With or without Jarrett, she didn't have to face decisions about this baby or her life all alone. She was going home.

A home where Jarrett didn't live.

Why did that make her chest ache?

She pulled her hand from his and started toward the bed, thinking to distract herself with the photographs once again. But Gray and Kathryn came through the door before she could take more than a step.

"I talked to Dr. Tiernan and the police," Gray told her. "There's no reason why you can't come home right now."

Beside him, Kathryn's smile beamed. "I called the airport. We can catch a flight out of Vancouver tonight. Barring any delays, we'll be home by mid-morning."

Ashley tried to smile at them, tried to feel something other than panic. She found herself turning to Jarrett. "Are you coming, as well? What about the conference that brought you up here?"

"The conference can go to hell." His brown eyes fairly danced. "We're taking you home to Texas, greatest state in the Union. The place where you belong."

When their plane landed in Amarillo, Ashley was to remember the way Jarrett had spoken of Texas. Like it was paradise. She mentally compared the arid landscape with the green trees and mountains visible from the hospital she had left behind, and she had to admit this dry, flat land spoke to her soul.

There was no time to ponder those feelings. A crowd met them at the airport. Ashley couldn't remember all the names. Jarrett's sister, Paige, her husband and four—or was it five?—children. Jarrett's father, a tall man with a booming voice and a face beaten to leather by sun and wind. There were Gray and Kathryn's daughters, eleven-year-old Lily and Whitney, a few years younger. Shy but eager to welcome her home, both of them regarded her with their father's sky-blue eyes.

Her brother Rick had the same eyes. But blond hair, like hers. She had been told he was a freshman at Texas Tech, in Lubbock, some distance to the south of Amarillo. Rick was tall and angular, handsome in a raw, youthful way. He grabbed her and shed his tears unashamed. He didn't seem to care that he was a complete stranger to her.

But she cared. She hated that she was frightened by people who only wanted to make her feel at home.

She hated that she clung to Jarrett's hand.

"Just remember how much they all love you," he told her on the drive from the airport.

Several more friends and neighbors waited at a long, rambling house of stone and stucco. These people babbled at her, introducing themselves, telling her their connection to her and her family, welcoming her home. No one said a word about the baby. They smiled, smiled, smiled, as if determined to be happy.

When they weren't talking in relentlessly cheerful voices, they ate and urged Ashley to do the same.

Tables groaned with food. Fried chicken. Barbecued pork. Corn on the cob. Potato salad. How was it that she could remember she loved chocolate cream pie when she didn't know her mother's maiden name or her brothers' birthdays?

Rick stuck close to Ashley's side. He pointed out the master-bedroom addition that had been built onto the house just last year. He took her to the barn, where several horses neighed a soft welcome, but prompted no answering recognition in Ashley. He introduced her to an aging beagle named Winks. He brought forward a parade of cats, all apparently descended from a feline Ashley had raised from a kitten. The hope in Rick's youthful features diminished each time Ashley said, "No, I don't remember."

When Kathryn finally dislodged Rick from Ashley's side, Gray stepped in. While he didn't press her as the younger man had, he didn't allow her even a breath of fresh air on her own. An arm's distance away was too much.

Only Jarrett's reassuring smile and the memory of his advice kept Ashley from screaming. She knew they all loved her. She should be happy.

But by late afternoon, her head was pounding from the noise, the intensity, the continuing failure of her mind to latch on to anything familiar.

She managed, finally, to escape her brothers, but fell into the clutches of a woman named Tillie who had commandeered the kitchen. Jarrett explained that Tillie had been his family's housekeeper since she was a baby. Obviously more than a mere employee, she had been left in charge of Lily and Whitney while Kathryn and Gray flew to Canada, and she was the source of the chocolate pie. Ashley imagined the thin, gray-haired matron was a terrific person under most circumstances. But not now, not when she clearly thought she was the one who could clear Ashley's memory. Ashley gratefully accepted her sister-in-law's help in making a getaway.

"Jarrett suggested you get some rest," Kathryn said, leading Ashley down a long hall. "I'm sorry everyone descended on the house this way. But their intentions are good. They all just want to give you a big Texas welcome-home."

"I'm fine, really. I appreciate everyone's concern."

"Jarrett said you barely slept on the plane."

"Too excited." Scared to death was more like it, Ashley said to herself.

Kathryn stopped in front of a door labeled with a sign marked Keep Out in bold red letters. "We're putting you in your old room. Lily's had it since you moved out, but she'll stay in the guest room."

"Oh, no. I don't want her put out of her room. Little girls that age are possessive of their space."

The other woman gave her a thoughtful look. "Is that how you felt at Lily's age?"

Ashley paused and tried to pinpoint just what she knew about girls Lily's age. She found the usual yawning black hole. The ache in her temples intensified. "I honestly have no idea how I know what little girls think or feel."

Kathryn patted her arm. "I guess some things are just instinctive."

"And my instincts tell me not to take Lily's room. Please."

"All right. She'll be happy. But let's take a look at her room, anyway. She has your furniture, the print you left hanging on the wall and some of your old stuffed animals. When we repainted, we used the same color you chose." Kathryn opened the door and stepped aside for Ashley.

The room was pink. A deep shade of dusty rose, against which the white French Provincial furniture looked both ornate and dainty. Filmy white curtains ruffled at the windows. On the wall facing the bed was a painting of a young girl with long blond hair. She was in profile, staring off across a rippling sea of grass, her beribboned hat clutched in her hands.

Ashley moved instinctively toward the framed print. Her throat tightened as a memory danced just beyond the reaches of her mind.

"The painting is familiar, isn't it, Ashe?"

At the sound of a male voice, she looked over to find Rick beside Kathryn. Jarrett was just behind him in the doorway.

When she didn't answer his question, Rick continued, "It's always been hanging in your room. For as long as I can remember. Don't you recognize the painting?"

The plea in his voice resonated deep inside Ashley. She looked at the painting again, hoping for a lightning bolt of recognition to sweep away the barrier between her and this memory.

As usual, she ran into that wall and went no further.

"Ashe?" Rick's yearning was heartbreakingly clear.

Gazing once again into his sincere blue eyes, Ashley couldn't find it within herself to disappoint him. So she lied. "I think…I do remember."

As thrilled as if she had recalled everything, Rick gave a whoop of triumph and rushed forward to grab her up and twirl her around.

Laughing in delight, Kathryn said, "When you first disappeared, Lily would say the girl in this painting was you, that you were somewhere in a beautiful field and you would come home when you were good and ready."

"I knew you would remember things here at home," Rick exclaimed, setting her on her feet again.

Only Jarrett was silent and watchful, leaning against the doorjamb, arms crossed.

"I'm going to tell Gray." Rick brushed past Jarrett and ran down the hall, calling for his brother.

"And I'm going to get the guest room ready." Kathryn gave Ashley a quick hug. "Are you sure you don't want to stay in here?"

"Very sure," Ashley whispered, not quite trusting her voice.

When Kathryn was gone, Ashley couldn't look at Jarrett. Eyes burning, she took a quick tour of the room. Touching the furry coat of a teddy bear. Inhaling a whiff of sweet, little-girl cologne.

Had she really dreamed in this canopied bed? Read by the light of that frilly lamp? God in heaven, this was such a beautiful, peaceful room. Why couldn't she remember the hours she had spent here?

"Ashley?"

She made herself face Jarrett.

"Lying won't make anything easier."

"It made Rick happy."

"And made you feel worse."

"It was one little lie." She rubbed her temples. "It gives them some hope that I'll someday be the person they remember."

Further discussion was halted by Gray's arrival and his excitement over her ridiculously tiny and totally false memory of the painting on the wall.

The effort of maintaining the lie sapped the last of Ashley's strength. Every muscle ached.

Rick showed her to a room decorated in soothing shades of green and blue. Kathryn was turning down the covers and had placed a nightgown across the foot of the bed. She showed Ashley some other clothes in a bureau drawer and in the closet. A full bath lay behind one of the room's doors.

"You used to love a good soak in the tub," Kathryn explained. "We're going to leave you alone to get some rest." She took Rick's arm and half led, half dragged him from the bedroom.

Ashley breathed a sigh of relief and eschewed the

tub for a quick shower and a change into fresh underwear and the borrowed nightgown.

Before slipping into bed, she closed the bedroom shades against the Texas sun. In the hospital, she had hated the night, but this sunshine was almost as bad. It burned so hot. And felt so strange. As odd and unfamiliar as this house, these people and her own skin.

Finally, she rolled onto her side and rubbed her stomach. When they told her at the hospital that she was pregnant, she had tried and failed to find some outward sign of her condition. But in only the past few days, she had detected a slight rounding of her belly. This child was growing.

This child. *Her* baby. A stranger, like its father. How she yearned to know how this child had been conceived. Surely it had been in love. She had to believe the beginning of this tiny new life had been tender. Not violent. Not sad.

But if that were so, where was the father? Why had she been alone in that small Canadian town? Alone and vulnerable enough to have been mugged. The questions gnawed at her, as they had from the beginning.

Eventually, Ashley slept. She dreamed of a street. Wet with rain. Cold. Empty. So dark even the light from the street lamps didn't reach the ground. She was lost and alone. Alone and afraid. Fear ripped at her, a beast with jagged teeth.

The beast jarred her awake, the same as every night.

Only tonight, Jarrett wasn't sitting by her bed, his hand on her arm, a ballast against this strange world.

In this warm, safe house that was her home, with people who loved her, all Ashley could think of was Jarrett.

Chapter Three

The next morning, Ashley selected some blue jeans and a cotton sweater from the clothes Kathryn had brought her in the hospital. She met the new day and her rediscovered family with her chin up and determination in her gut. Gathered en masse around the kitchen table for breakfast, the family greeted her with effusive, but uncertain welcome.

Rick needed to get back to school in Lubbock, but he hung around for a full hour, telling her stories he wanted her to remember until she thought she would scream. The disappointment in his gaze hurt her deeply.

Gray was solicitous, tentative. Worry marred the handsome planes of his face. Ashley wanted to reassure him, tell him her memory would soon return. But she couldn't make promises she couldn't keep. Besides, he was a stranger. She hardly knew what to say to him.

Only Kathryn and her daughters, Lily and Whitney, seemed to understand that Ashley needed space. The girls went off to school. Kathryn shooed Rick out the door, as well, and was working on getting her husband off to his veterinary clinic when Jarrett came driving up.

Gray's eyes narrowed at the sight of Jarrett. But Ashley ignored her brother's reaction. She was inordinately relieved to see Jarrett again. His tall, strong form inspired the only real confidence she felt about her situation. She didn't want to cling to him. More than anything, she wanted to be strong and brave and independent. Yet just seeing him brought her an incredible sense of calm.

"I'm staying here for a while, out at the ranch with Dad and Tillie," Jarrett announced once Kathryn had sat him down and poured a cup of coffee. "The partners in my practice are covering for me for the next week or so."

Ashley's relief was marred only by Gray's disapproving grunt. Kathryn shot her husband a warning glance.

Jarrett ignored him and turned to Ashley. "What do you want to do today?"

"I think she should rest," Gray stated before she could reply. "Give herself a chance to settle in."

"I thought she'd probably want to get out and see the place she called home," Jarrett said.

Gray set his coffee cup down with a decisive thump. "We can take her around when she's ready."

"But I planned—" Jarrett started to say.

"But you don't—" Gray said at the same time.

"That's enough." Kathryn cut them both off with her gentle admonishment and the touch of her hands on their arms. She quelled another eruption from Gray with a glance that brooked no argument. "You two are overwhelming Ashley. Aren't they?" she added, turning to her sister-in-law.

Ashley shifted uncertainly in her chair. She didn't want to hurt her brother or Jarrett, but she hated the way they talked about her as if she weren't here. She didn't understand the tension that ran, heavy as steel, between the two men.

"What do you want?" Gray asked her, looking disgruntled but resigned.

"For you all just to be normal," she said quickly. At the glance that passed among the others, she laughed softly. "I know *normalcy* is not a word that really applies to this crazy situation. But please…I want everyone just to go about their lives. Gray, you and Kathryn should just go to work. Just like usual."

Gray's voice roughened with disapproval. "We're not leaving you here alone."

"I'll stay with her," Jarrett said. "Won't let her out of my sight."

Gray looked as if he feared Jarrett's presence more than leaving Ashley on her own. But Kathryn talked him into going to work. She left soon after to attend to business at her bridal boutique. Ashley caught a mischievous glint in Kathryn's gaze as she said goodbye to her and Jarrett, but she wasn't sure what that meant.

And then they were alone. In the quiet kitchen. Where a clock ticked softly, a refrigerator hummed. Where Ashley suddenly found it hard to meet Jarrett's gaze.

After a few moments of uncomfortable silence had passed, he stood and put out his hand. "Come on. Let's get out of here."

She hesitated, thinking of Gray's disapproval.

But Jarrett would have none of that. "Come on. I've got a lot to show you."

Putting her hand in his felt completely right. Totally natural. So they locked up the house and were soon tooling down a flat Texas two-lane road in the aging Jeep that Jarrett had borrowed from his family's ranch.

The wind blew Ashley's hair back from her face. The sun was warm on her bare arms. And when Jarrett sped up to pass a slow-moving tractor trailer, her stomach jumped with excitement. He laughed out loud, and so did she, their gazes meeting, holding. Not like strangers. Not like strangers at all.

"Where are we going?" she asked above the sound of the tires and the wind.

"Wherever the road takes us." His smile was a brilliant slash in his handsome face. Slightly dangerous. Totally exhilarating.

Ashley sat back, content to let him take her where he wanted.

They spent most of the day wandering the back roads. Jarrett pointed out places they had gone before. A roadside dive where Ashley had once drank too many beers on top of too many tacos. The creekside parking area where they used to come to make out. The rutted back entrance to the expansive Double M Ranch, which his grandfather had founded.

They ate lunch with Jarrett's father, Rex, and with Tillie. That afternoon, Jarrett got Ashley up on a horse. A gentle roan he said had always been one of her favorites. He mounted a black stallion, and they cantered for a lazy hour.

Ashley arrived home weary, slightly sunburned and smiling. She realized that for most of the day, Jarrett had made no demands on her, asked no questions, nor had he peered at her as if to gauge whether her memories were being sparked.

Gray was waiting at home. He was furious, though he managed to hide his anger from Ashley pretty well. Once she said goodbye to Jarrett, however, and went in the house, Gray opened up. He couldn't believe Jarrett, a doctor, had allowed Ashley to ride after the blow to the head she had received in the mugging.

"What's wrong with you?" Gray demanded. "What do you mean being so damn irresponsible?"

Jarrett's hands clenched into fists at his sides, but he silently counted to ten before replying to Gray. He knew the man was reacting to the relief of having

Ashley home—safe and sound at long last. Gray wanted to guard her. Protect her. God knew, Jarrett wanted to do the same. But he knew keeping her locked in the house wasn't the way to heal her broken mind. She had to start living again. Right away. For her own sake. And for the sake of the child she carried.

For her sake, Jarrett made himself ignore Gray's anger and insults. "I'm going home," he told Gray. "I'll be back tomorrow morning. To take Ashley to a doctor's appointment I set up with Kathryn's OB in town."

Gray sputtered. Jarrett walked away. He'd be damned if he let the man keep him from Ashley. She needed Jarrett, and for his part in whatever had happened to her, he owed her his support. Gray was going to have to accept that much.

The next few days fell into a rhythm for Ashley. The early mornings and evenings she spent with Kathryn, Gray and the girls. Rick called every night. A few old friends, none of whom she could remember, stopped in as well. But those meetings were awkward for all concerned. They didn't know what to say, and Ashley didn't remember them.

Every other available moment was spent with Jarrett. These were the only times she could really relax. He made few demands on her. He didn't quiz with Rick's youthful zest. Or watch her with Gray's trepidation. Jarrett didn't seem disappointed that few memories were trickling back from her past. He was simply there, steady and reassuring.

And fun. He made her laugh. He told her crazy things they had done together when they were younger. He even talked about the baby. Simply. Naturally. Without the hushed tone that crept into Gray's voice when he mentioned the child.

Kathryn's OB confirmed what the doctors in Canada had said: all signs indicated her pregnancy was normal. With Jarrett at her side, they viewed the tape of the ultrasound performed at the hospital. The doctor pointed out the faint outline of the fetus. In another few weeks, they would do another ultrasound. Until then, Ashley was to proceed with a normal life.

As normal a life as an amnesiac could have, that is.

Her biggest problem was Gray. Especially his animosity toward Jarrett. Gray wanted Jarrett to go back to Dallas. She knew that was inevitable, and she dreaded the day. Yet she had no claim on Jarrett. While they had once been engaged, that had ended before she left here and disappeared. Clearly, she had moved on. The child growing in her womb was evidence of that much.

The child. *Her* child. Ashley struggled hard to overcome the sense of disconnectedness she felt toward her baby. Even the slight bowing of her stomach and the tiny taped image on the monitor at the doctor's office didn't make much of an impact.

Her child was almost as unreal as the rest of the shadowed details of the life she had forgotten.

Thursday, Ashley turned in early. She was head-achy and tired, but she couldn't settle down. Finally, when the house was quiet, she pulled on a robe and went to the family room, hoping a television program might lull her to sleep. In the dim golden glow from a solitary lamp, she found Kathryn, with Whitney cuddled on her lap asleep.

"Poor kid's having a restless night." With a gen-tle, loving hand, Kathryn stroked her youngest's dark hair. "She's too big for this babying, but sometimes she just needs to be held. And when she's this way, I never can get her to stay in bed."

"There's been too much upheaval this week for a little girl to take in easily."

"I think she just had too many chocolate-chip cookies before bed."

The two women shared a chuckle, and Whitney stirred, burrowing even closer to her mother. Kathryn crooned in comfort.

Ashley was overcome with yearning. She wished her own troubles could be erased with a soft touch and a few soothing words. There might have been a time when she would have curled up next to Kathryn and poured out the secrets of her heart. More than her memories, she hated having lost her ease with these people who loved her. People she should love in return. A family whose members were still little more than strangers.

As if she had read Ashley's mind, Kathryn invited, "Sit down with us." She gestured toward the other end of the overstuffed sofa.

"I don't want to keep Whitney awake by talking. You need to get some sleep, as well."

Kathryn laid her cheek against her daughter's hair. "She's content and I'm fine for now. Sit down and tell me why you're up."

Sighing, Ashley curled into the plump, comfortable cushions. She gave a wry smile. "I wouldn't know where to start on the list of reasons I can't sleep."

"Are Gray and Jarrett on that list?"

Ashley had to laugh. "No mystery there."

Kathryn sighed. "Unfortunately, the two of them are simply running true to form. Two big, muleheaded men who think they know best for the people in their lives."

"Gray wants Jarrett to disappear."

"He's been wanting that since Jarrett first stepped into your life, when you were seventeen."

At Ashley's groan, Kathryn went on to explain, "It would have been the same with any man. You know Gray became the head of the household when you were only eleven, when Rick was a baby."

"When our mother died." Ashley idly stroked the bracelet on her wrist. Other than the vague impressions that had come to her the day Jarrett told her the bracelet had been her mother's, she still couldn't recall anything about the woman who had brought her into the world, who had nurtured her as she was now nurturing the child in her womb. Her mother was as much an enigma as every other part of her life.

Kathryn continued, ''Gray took on big responsibilities when he was just out of his teens. He became way overprotective of you and Rick. When it was time for you to spread your wings, he kept trying to keep you in a gilded cage, safe from harm, from hurt. He's always blamed himself for your disappearance.''

Ashley was surprised. ''I thought he blamed Jarrett.''

''Oh, yes,'' Kathryn agreed. ''Gray definitely faults Jarrett for breaking your heart and sending you off to disappear. But he faults himself for not keeping you away from Jarrett.''

''Could he have kept me away from Jarrett?''

Kathryn laughed out loud. ''Ashley, my dear, from the time I met you, you were hell-bent on doing exactly as you pleased, when you pleased, how you pleased. And Gray was hell-bent on keeping you out of harm's way. You and he were on a collision course.''

''But by the time I left here I was a grown woman, not some rebellious teenager.''

''A grown woman who had just up and moved to Dallas to be with Jarrett, a move that infuriated Gray.''

''Because he hates Jarrett,'' Ashley murmured.

Kathryn shook her head. ''He doesn't hate him. Not really. He simply thought Jarrett was wrong for you, that he would hurt you.''

''And he thinks that still.''

Kathryn shrugged. "The important thing is—what do you think about Jarrett?"

Surprised, Ashley blinked.

Her sister-in-law laughed. "I guess that's a strange question for me to ask you, considering you don't quite know what to think about anything."

"Well..." Ashley thrust a hand through her long heavy hair. "I'm not sure what you mean by asking what I think about Jarrett. I mean...he's so kind. So patient and understanding. I think he's...fine." The word sounded silly and insubstantial, a poor choice for what she felt.

"Yes, he is all that," Kathryn agreed, her gaze watchful, cautious. "You used to love him."

An ache started in Ashley's chest. She couldn't help asking, "Did he love me the same way?"

Kathryn nodded.

"Then it's a pity we let it slip away."

"Maybe it's not gone. You did remember his name when he walked into that hospital room. And he does care."

Before she could let Kathryn's wishful thinking suck her in, Ashley shook her head. "Jarrett is simply being kind to me. It's preposterous to even think about anything more. Not when I'm still so lost within myself. Not when I'm pregnant with some other man's child. Some man who could be waiting for me, somewhere."

"Is that really what you believe?" Kathryn asked, her own doubts clear.

Because that question cut too close to her fears,

Ashley ignored her and got to her feet. "I'm going back to bed. Good night."

Hard as she tried not to think about issues Kathryn had raised, Ashley was still going over the conversation the next morning, just after breakfast. The girls had left for school and Gray for his clinic. Kathryn, who took Friday mornings off from her boutique, was straightening the kitchen while Ashley made her bed.

Ashley expected Jarrett to arrive sometime this morning, but she wasn't adverse to a few hours alone. She knew she was coming to depend on him. Surely that couldn't be right or healthy. Soon he would go home. She had a life to live that was separate and apart from his. She had a child....

"Stop it," she said aloud to the empty bedroom. She didn't feel like rehashing the obvious.

To distract herself, she opened the closet doors. Kathryn had told her earlier this week that there were boxes of her belongings stored here. Every day, Ashley had promised herself she would look through those tangible scraps of the past. Every day, she found an excuse not to. Well, not anymore.

With determination, she dragged the neatly labeled boxes from the closet. In the first, she found school-day mementos. Grade cards and faded certificates for spelling and English. Dried corsages and yellowing ticket stubs from movies and concerts. Photographs of many of the people who had visited her this week. Lots of pictures of Jarrett.

In another box, she found a stack of letters that

bore his name in the return address. Beneath them was a journal where Jarrett's presence and importance in her life were spelled out in bad poetry and dramatic prose that leaped out at her as she leafed through the pages. The evidence of her youthful passion made Ashley smile. And ache. She set the letters and journal aside and reached for the last of the boxes.

Inside was a plastic zippered garment bag stamped with golden letters which read Blue Heaven Weddings. The name of Kathryn's wedding boutique. Ashley's mouth went dry. She almost shoved the bag back in the box and the box back in the closet. But her curiosity was too strong. So she slid the zipper down and pulled a dress out of the protective tissue.

A wedding dress, of course. An off-the shoulder bodice covered in lace. A swirl of chiffon over a silk underskirt embroidered with flowers and sparkling with beads and sequins. A breathtaking, top-of-the-cake, romantic dream of a dress.

Ashley couldn't stop herself. She turned to the gilt-framed mirror that hung over the dresser and held the dress up in front of her. She stared at her reflection for a long, long time.

Behind her, Jarrett's reflection appeared in the mirror.

Ashley sucked in her breath, but didn't move. What was he thinking? Feeling? This was the dress she had bought to wear to their wedding. Even if he had never seen it before, he knew what this dress represented.

His dark-eyed gaze remained steady on hers in the mirror. His voice was deep, faintly troubled. "You left this dress in Dallas."

Confused, she turned to face him, still holding the gown in front of her. "Dallas?"

"We were going to elope. You brought the dress. When we argued over postponing the wedding, you left it behind."

Jarrett reached out and touched a frill of lace. "That was one reason I thought you'd come straight back. To get this dress."

"But I didn't come back."

He shook his head. "I brought it here, asked Kathryn to put it away for you."

Ashley ran a hand down the silky skirt. "It's beautiful."

"You don't remember buying it?" This was the first time all week that Jarrett had pushed her for a memory.

She wished with all her heart she could give it to him. But she couldn't.

He sighed, started to speak, then obviously reconsidered. Finally, he said, "You'll remember, Ashe. Someday, you will remember the day you bought this dress. The way you felt. The plans you were making." His tone was filled with determination.

"I wish I could be so certain," Ashley murmured.

Jarrett lifted his hand to her cheek. His fingertips were gentle against her skin. "I am certain—that's for sure," he said with complete and total confidence. "Just as I never lost hope that you'd come home, I know you'll remember everything. You'll get it all back. And you'll be just fine.''

The moment was magical. Electric. Full of promise and hope. As delicate and beautiful as the lace on the dress she clasped to her bosom.

Ashley felt that if she swayed forward. Just a fraction of an inch. That Jarrett would kiss her.

And, oh, how she wanted him to kiss her. That desire snaked into her heart. Forbidden. Reckless. Probably foolish. But strong enough to make her chest ache.

In the end, Kathryn called from the hall outside the bedroom. Ashley stepped back. Jarrett left to help Kathryn rescue one of the cats from a tree in the backyard.

Ashley put the dress away, burying its box beneath the carton filled with school keepsakes and the letters and journal. Maybe someday she would go through them again. Maybe something there would spark a memory.

Right now, those cartons were a dead end. As unlikely to unlock her mind as her thickening waist was to fit into that dress. Even though Jarrett's faith had paid off and she was home, she wasn't the same girl who had read those letters and written in that journal.

Ashley lived, but the girl she had been was dead.

Who was the woman who had taken her place?

Discovering her identity was what Ashley should be thinking of. Not lace and chiffon. Not candles and kisses. Definitely not how Jarrett's mouth would feel against her own.

Chapter Four

Jarrett had to return to Dallas on Sunday. Leaving Ashley bothered him more than he liked to admit to himself. Every morning of the two weeks they were apart, he told himself he should be content to at least know where she was. But the fact that he couldn't see to her welfare himself ate at him. Every night, he gave in to curiosity and concern and called her.

He sensed her growing frustration and her impatience with herself. As the days slipped past and only the most insignificant of memories came back to her, she felt she was letting her family down. Jarrett feared Gray and Rick were pushing her too hard to remember. Not wanting to duplicate their mistakes, he steered his conversations with Ashley away from the past. He suggested several books, a movie, a favorite television program she might enjoy. She responded with palpable relief. The rapport that had always been between them was surprisingly unchanged.

He called in every favor owed him to get the next weekend off to return to Amarillo. Friday afternoon he caught a plane, rented a car and drove straight to Gray and Kathryn's home.

The October air was warm, even by Texas's mild autumn standards, when Jarrett stepped out of the car's air-conditioned comfort. His wristwatch showed five o'clock, so there was a full hour or so of daylight remaining. By the looks of the clouds on the horizon, they would have rain sometime tonight, possibly even a thunderstorm. He shed his jacket and tie, headed for the back door and entered without bothering to knock, a habit born of his hundreds of visits to this house.

As he expected, the family was gathered in the cheerful, noisy kitchen. No one even noticed him. A small television set was playing to a disinterested audience. Eight-year-old Whitney's dark head was bent over a puzzle at the table, while a half-grown cat played with the frayed laces of her tennis shoes. Gray, his back to the door, was on the phone in the doorway to the hall. Kathryn was assembling ingredients for a salad and listening to her older daughter complain about being grounded from a slumber party that apparently every other girl in her class was attending.

Ashley was nowhere in sight.

Jarrett cleared his throat. "A guy could make off with all your livestock, and nobody in this house would hear a thing."

Four heads swiveled in his direction. The girls, to whom he was a part of the family, greeted him with wide smiles. Gray frowned, but ended his phone call. Kathryn turned off the television.

Jarrett asked, "Where's Ashe?"

"Outside somewhere," Lily said.

Whitney added, "Down by the creek, I think."

When the girls had scurried off, he faced Gray and Kathryn. "How's everything going?"

Gray shrugged.

"You seem upset," Jarrett said.

Kathryn shot her husband a warning glance before he could make a reply. "We're just a little frustrated. Ashley is, too. She thought, like we all did, that her being at home would bring her memory back."

"It's only been three weeks since we found her."

With a short laugh, Gray said, "As you know, patience has never been a virtue of most of the people in this family."

"An understatement if I ever heard one," Jarrett agreed.

"Ashley wants to know who she is and what's happened to her. Right now." Kathryn centered her gaze on Jarrett. "I don't know what will happen if she doesn't have some kind of breakthrough soon."

"It's unlikely she won't remember." Jarrett didn't want to give them false hope, but he didn't think it was time to push the panic button, either. "Did she see the psychologist today?" He had recommended a therapist, whom Ashley had already seen several times. She talked little about the sessions when he called, and he had not pushed.

"Ashley's appointment was this afternoon," Gray said, his brow knitting. "And she hasn't said ten words since I picked her up afterward. She said she doesn't want dinner and went off by herself. From what I can tell, Ashley is worse instead of better."

"Oh, Gray," Kathryn chided him. "She's had only a few sessions with this psychologist. What do you want, a miracle?"

"I want her well and whole. I want all of this to never have happened," Gray retorted, glaring at Jarrett.

"But it did happen," Kathryn said. "And we've got to help her. Most of all, we have to give her some space. She's not a child. She doesn't need all of us breathing down her neck."

"We're her family," Gray protested.

Kathryn's features narrowed. Jarrett got the distinct impression this wasn't the first time she and her husband had argued about giving Ashley some time to herself.

Dull red stained Gray's neck. "We're trying to help her."

"You and Rick—"

"Where is Rick?" Jarrett interjected, hoping to forestall a confrontation.

"Ashley told him he should stay in Lubbock this

weekend." The glance Kathryn sent in Gray's direction dared him to interrupt. "She doesn't want Rick giving up his life at college to come running home to be with her all the time."

Gray's jaw squared. "She hurt Rick by asking him to stay away. I don't know why she can't understand how much he wants and needs to be with her."

"Rick has to respect her need for some freedom," Kathryn protested. "We all do. She's already got the four of us surrounding her all the time. Plus well-meaning friends and neighbors. I swear, if Tillie bakes her another chocolate cream pie…"

Jarrett held up a hand to stop Gray's protest. This argument was pointless. "At the risk of being another person breathing down her neck, I'm going to find Ashley."

"She misses you," Kathryn said.

"Even though you call every night." It was clear Gray didn't like that one bit.

"She hasn't asked me not to call," Jarrett said.

That comment elicited a warning from Gray. "You be careful with her."

Gray's voice deepened. "I'm just putting you on notice. You hurt Ashley now, and I'll kill you with my bare hands."

"Gray!" Kathryn protested.

Because he knew staying would lead to a full-scale argument with Gray, Jarrett headed out the door and toward the creek where Whitney had indicated he might find Ashley. His long, angry strides carried him across the yard. While he resented Gray's continuing and pointless disapproval, what he hated most was the knowledge that the man had good reason to distrust him. Gray blamed Jarrett for Ashley's situation. Almost as much as Jarrett blamed himself.

By God, he had to make things right.

He walked off his anger as he crossed the pasture toward the line of trees on the horizon. The stand of cottonwood, thinning branches framed against darkening clouds, marked the edge of Gray's property and the creek. Jarrett spotted Ashley sitting beneath one of those trees. He called out a greeting.

She scrambled to her feet, brushing dirt and leaves from her tight, gray bike shorts. Her hair had been cut and fell in a heavy sweep of gold to a point just below her chin. The change highlighted her unusual eyes and the gentle curves of her mouth. Before he hugged her, Jarrett noted another change—the slight belling of her stomach beneath an old Texas Tech T-shirt. Incredibly enough, he could tell a change from less than two weeks ago.

"I didn't know if you would really come," she said, pulling away.

"I told you last night on the phone that I was coming."

"But you're so busy."

"The good thing about being in practice with other doctors is that you can generally find someone to cover for you."

"I'm glad you're here." Ashley's smile was as welcome as the breeze that set the drying leaves rattling on the trees above them.

"You always liked this spot." Jarrett drew her toward a large flat rock resting at the top of the creek bank. The creek was more a trickle than a stream, testament to another dry autumn in West Texas.

Ashley gave the rock a wary glance. "I heard something rustling over here a while ago. I thought it could be a snake. Gray started warning me about rattlers the first time I went for a walk by myself." Her impatience with Gray's protectiveness rang through the words.

"No need to worry." Just as a precaution, Jarrett picked up a stick and stirred a pile of leaves and gravel near the base of the rock.

"The way Gray makes it sound, there are all sorts of predators just waiting to strike me down. He doesn't want me going anywhere alone."

Jarrett laughed. "He's too happy having you home to take any chances, I guess."

After following him up on the rock and taking a seat, Ashley said, "Gray's not happy with me. Not at all."

"He's worried."

She gave Jarrett a sidelong look. "What did he say to you?"

No good would come of sharing all of Gray's outburst with her. "He's a little impatient for your memory to come back."

"A little?" Ashley cocked an eyebrow at the understatement and laughed. Jarrett realized he hadn't heard her laughter for far too long.

He grinned at her. "Nobody laughs like you do, Ashe."

"Dr. Duval says I have to start trying to laugh more. She says I have to take joy where I find it."

"She's right." Jarrett tossed the stick toward the creek. "Do you like her?"

"She's okay."

"I sense some hesitation there."

"She's not doing me any good."

He chuckled again. "You're as bad as Gray, dismissing the value of therapy after just a few sessions."

A moment of silence passed before Ashley spoke again. "I'll tell you what I told her this afternoon." She took a breath before continuing. "I'm afraid I don't want my memory to return."

Biting back an instinctive denial, Jarrett took some time before replying. "I don't believe you would consciously not want to recall your life."

"I didn't say it was a conscious holding back. It's more…" She bowed her head. "There's some reason that my mind decided to blank out. Maybe I'm better off not remembering what that was. Only trouble is, my stupid brain took all the good stuff away, too. My family. My friends. Losing those memories is the price I'm paying for keeping the rotten ones buried."

She turned her luminous amber eyes to him again. "My brain has taken everything that makes me myself. It's frustrating. Everyone is always telling me that I'm acting like myself or that I'm choosing to wear a color that I've always loved or listening to a song that was a favorite. Gray and Kathryn, Rick, you, even Tillie—they all know more about me than me.''

''They're just trying to help you.''

''I'm not faulting anyone. But there's this part of me that keeps wondering what all of them will do if it turns out that I never remember.''

''That wouldn't be the end of the world.''

''That's what I tell myself. I decided the past was over and done with and I had to concentrate on the future....'' Absently, she touched her stomach, though she didn't speak of the child.

''Looking forward sounds very positive.''

''But everyone here needs me to remember, needs me to be the person I was.'' She twisted around to face him. ''But I know that whatever and whenever I remember, or even if I don't, I'm going to be a different person than they all want me to be.''

''Everyone changes. Even if you had just been away for three years, without the memory loss, you still would have changed.''

''I don't believe my family is ever going to understand that. It's not so much Kathryn, of course, but Gray and Rick. For me to have changed too much frightens them. I believe they're every bit as afraid of what happened to me as I am. At the same time, they're desperate for me to remember the life I had before I left here.''

''If you remember what they want you to, you'll probably remember what they don't want to know.''

She blew out a frustrated breath. "A mixed-up mess, isn't it?"

"Your mind has played you a dirty trick. It stinks, too, because you don't deserve it."

Suddenly agitated, she pushed herself to her feet. "It's hard to say what I deserve, given that we don't have a clue where I've been or what I've done these past three years."

"Nothing you could have done could make you deserve this."

"I wish I could be as sure as you." She turned and jumped from the rock, her shoulders straight as she headed across the field.

With several long strides, he reached her side. "It's not important what you did or didn't do during the past three years. You've said yourself there's probably a good reason you don't want to remember. Just accept that for now and go on."

She stopped and faced him. "You think I can pretend I was born the day I woke up in the hospital?"

"Maybe not entirely—"

"Of course I can't." She touched her stomach again. "There is this small complication. If my memory doesn't return, how am I going to answer when this child asks about its father?"

"Don't worry about that now."

She seemed not to hear him. Her voice more angry than tearful, she pressed both hands to her stomach. "This child growing inside me could be any man's baby. What am I going to tell this child?"

"Is the father all you can think about?" Jarrett

placed his hands on Ashley's shoulders. "How about just thinking about the mother?"

A line appeared between Ashley's delicate brows. "What are you saying?"

"Stop worrying about what you don't know. Follow through on the decision you made to keep looking ahead."

"But this child—"

"*This* child is *your* child."

He silenced her protest by placing his fingers lightly against her lips. "Not once have I heard you say anything about not having this baby."

Her eyes grew wide. "They talked to me about that at the hospital, but something inside me just couldn't consider not having my child."

"And you're not talking like you'll be giving the baby away, either."

She hesitated, stepping backward. "I'm not...no, of course not."

"So you're going to have this child, raise this child, *your* child."

Very slowly she nodded.

"Just by making those decisions, you were looking ahead, investing yourself in hope for the future." The light breeze blew a strand of her hair across her face. Jarrett gently brushed it back, his knuckles grazing her soft cheek. "You keep saying you're a different person. But deciding to have this baby, to keep it—those are the sort of choices you always would have made."

"Are you sure?"

"Of course I am. Your mind may be playing tricks, but it can't disguise the person you really are. Little by little, the real you is coming out. Once Gray and Rick see that, they'll be fine with what you can and can't recall about the past. And you'll deal with it, no matter what. Ashley Grant never ran from her problems."

"That's not true. I ran away and disappeared."

"I forced you into that," he muttered, his voice harsh even to his own ears. "That's different from running."

"I hate the way that makes me sound," she protested. "Like this weak namby-pamby who ran off in a snit."

The muscles worked in his throat. "You were in a snit, but that was my fault. I handled you all wrong."

Ashley frowned at his choice of words. "*Handled* me? I thought we argued."

"Because we needed to postpone the wedding."

Again, she was puzzled. She didn't like the picture of her painted by his description of the way they had parted. Like someone in need of guidance, who couldn't make decisions for herself. "You're saying we *needed* to postpone the wedding? The way I understood it, you got cold feet."

His brow wrinkled. "Yes, but—"

Abruptly, Ashley cut off his explanation with a sharp intake of breath. Her hands pressed to her stomach.

"What is it?" Jarrett demanded.

"It's the baby. It's..." She lifted her gaze to his, amazed by the sensations inside her. "I think I feel my baby."

"You're kidding?" Eyes widening, Jarrett's gaze dropped to her stomach. "Is this the first time? How does it feel?"

"Like bubbles. Here." Without pausing to think, she took his hand and guided it under her T-shirt, low on her belly. His broad palm and long fingers were warm against the thin knit of her tight shorts. Beneath them, Ashley felt her baby's tiny, fluttering movements.

"Do you feel that?" she demanded.

Jarrett laughed. "Of course not. You're barely more than four months along. I doubt I could feel anything."

"It's going crazy in there. All day long, I've had this funny tingling feeling, but I didn't think...it didn't occur to me that it was my baby."

"How could you know?"

"I know, but—" Suddenly alarmed, she clutched his hand harder against her. "You don't think there's anything wrong, do you?"

"If there's no pain—"

"Just bubbles—"

"Could just be gas."

She swatted at him playfully. "Don't be crude, Dr. McMullen."

"Well, you know me...." The words trailed away, and guilt replaced amusement in his expression. "But you don't know me."

Ashley snapped out of the spell brought on by the movements of her child. She realized how naturally she had placed Jarrett's hand on her, how intimately his fingers were still splayed across her stomach, over her child. She wanted to move away. Yet she didn't want to move. Except perhaps closer to him. She followed her impulse.

His lips settled against hers in a gesture that felt as effortless as breathing. His mouth was firm, undemanding and yet full of promise. He nibbled at her lips, skimmed them with his tongue, a coaxing pressure no woman in her right mind could fail to answer. Ashley opened her lips for his soft invasion. She sighed, leaning into the kiss. Nothing she had done since coming to in the hospital had felt as right as this. Despite all her best efforts, she had been thinking about kissing him for weeks. The reality lived up to all her speculations.

But abruptly, Jarrett pulled back, his hand jerking away from her stomach. His brown eyes were wide with dismay. "I'm sorry, I shouldn't have—"

"No, it's okay."

"But I shouldn't…we shouldn't…" He swallowed hard. "Hell, Ashe, we both know this isn't a good idea."

Face flaming, she murmured her agreement. Of course he was right. There was no reason why a successful young doctor who had written her off years ago should invest anything more of himself in a woman carrying another man's baby.

Jarrett jammed his hands in the pockets of his suit pants, as if he didn't know what else to do with them.

"Let's just pretend it didn't happen," she suggested.

He looked as uncertain of success as she felt.

"We just got caught up in the moment, in the baby."

His gaze dropped once again to her belly.

To avoid looking at him, she filled the awkward silence with chatter. "I hadn't felt the baby at all, and I know Kathryn was beginning to worry."

"But there's no need for that. He's fine. Just fine. And all yours."

"Mine. My baby." She drew in a deep breath and found herself looking into Jarrett's eyes, after all. A goofy, ridiculous grin tugged at the corners of her mouth. His smile looked just as giddy. She breathed a sigh of relief, glad their unexpected kiss hadn't ruined the rapport that seemed to come so easily to them. She didn't have his ease with anyone else.

Still grinning, he took her hand and started toward the house. "Come on. It's getting dark out here. Let's go tell Gray and Kathryn. They'll be relieved to see you smiling."

Ashley wanted to protest. For some reason, she wished they could keep this moment all to themselves. A foolish notion, she knew, but she couldn't stop it.

These past two weeks, she had been very strict with herself where Jarrett was concerned. When he called, she kept her equilibrium. She told herself he was simply being kind, checking in to see that she was okay. Like a good friend. Not an ex-fiancé. She had imagined kissing him, yes, but for the most part, she had kept those thoughts under control.

What had passed between them was simply shared awe at the miracle of the tiny life moving inside her. She had infected him with her excitement. He had kissed her. Much as he had probably kissed her hundreds of times in the past. What was new and exciting to her was nothing more than habit to him.

As they headed for the house, she wondered how many times he had kissed her. Would she ever remember? Did she want to? Or was it new memories she wanted to make with this tall, solid man with the arresting smile and impossibly tousled hair?

She had been so upset earlier today. Her world seemed hopeless. A half hour with Jarrett changed her whole perspective. That knowledge was as reassuring as it was dangerous.

The sun was setting, streaking the thickening clouds to the west with gold and purple. The breeze carried the scents of earth and an impending change in the weather. A horse neighed from the corral beside the barn. Lights bloomed from the windows of the house.

Ashley saw Gray come to the back-porch door, his silhouette broad and solid against the light. No doubt he would be displeased to see her with Jarrett. But even that knowledge couldn't dispel the peace she was feeling in her heart.

For the first time since he had brought her home,

she felt the need to see Gray. She waved and called his name. Holding the screened door open, he waited for them on the top porch step.

She hurried forward, up the steps and flung her arms around her brother.

His hesitation was momentary before his arms closed around her.

"I felt the baby," she whispered. "Gray, I felt my baby move."

Years fell away from Gray's features. Calling out for his wife and daughters, he tugged Ashley toward the kitchen.

In a moment, she was surrounded by Kathryn and the girls, enveloped by their excited questions and laughter.

She felt loved. Warmed by the reality of her child. The feeling was so intense, so gratifying, she turned to share it with Jarrett, to draw him into the circle of what finally felt like a real family to her. Grinning, he slipped an arm around her waist.

She sensed Gray's disapproval, but she would have none of that tonight. For whatever reason, she needed, wanted Jarrett here with her, and no one was going to stop her.

As usual, Kathryn eased the tension in the air. "The girls want to make ice-cream sundaes. Everybody want some?"

"Sure," Ashley said, turning to Whitney and Lily with a smile.

Jarrett agreed. "I want hot fudge. How about you guys?"

When everyone was gathered around the table, Ashley did her best to ignore the undercurrents flashing between Jarrett and Gray by concentrating on her nieces. As had been the case since she came home, the girls provided a welcome distraction.

Unlike their father and their Uncle Rick, the two girls didn't have many expectations of Ashley. Lily, especially, remembered her very well, but with the flexibility of the young, she accepted that her aunt had changed. Interestingly enough, both Lily and Whitney were more respectful of Ashley's need for privacy and independence than either Gray or Rick.

Gray underscored that point once his daughters took themselves off to the family room to watch a video. He turned to Ashley and with forced casualness, said, "So, I guess you're tired, right? It's been a long day." Clearly he was implying Jarrett should leave.

"I'm just fine," Ashley said, feeling a sharp pinch of temper.

Her brother blinked. "You seemed wrung out after the therapy session this afternoon."

"But I'm fine now."

"Are you sure?"

"Gray, please," Kathryn murmured. "Must you badger her?"

His features hardened. "Just because I'm concerned about her well-being is no reason to get mad at me."

Ashley felt a spurt of anger and spoke without

thinking. "Your brand of caring can be pretty damn suffocating."

Gray's brows lowered.

Ashley saw Jarrett and Kathryn exchange a guarded glance. She didn't want to fight, didn't want to hurt Gray. He loved her. His joy when she met him at the door with a hug had spoken louder than words about how much he cared. But he was simply driving her insane.

Her motions slow and deliberate, she pushed away from the table and carried her bowl to the kitchen sink. "I think I'd like to get out for a while, go for a drive. With Jarrett." The challenge in her words was impossible to ignore, as was the straightforward way she faced her brother.

"It's late," Gray replied. "I'm sure the good doctor here..." He flicked a glance toward Jarrett. "I'm sure he's worn out from his trip home."

Ashley felt her cheeks flush. "Gray, are you trying to tell me I can't go for a simple drive?"

"What I'm trying to do—"

"Is control me," she countered.

"I want to protect you."

"You want to lock me up." Ashley's voice rose. "I'm an adult, carrying a child, and you're trying to send me to my room like some ten-year-old."

Gray rose. "Now, you just listen—"

But the sound of laughter cut him off. Kathryn was shaking with mirth, tears running down her face. And Jarrett was doing little better.

"What the hell—?" Gray sputtered.

Kathryn choked out an explanation. "I'm sorry. I know I shouldn't laugh. But you two sound just like yourselves, like you did the first time I met you both. Ashley pushing for independence and Gray trying to hold on. It sounds so familiar, so…right."

Gray's face took on a purplish tinge. Ashley's jaw set.

Jarrett laughed harder. "Kathryn is so right. It's just like the first time I ever picked Ashley up for a date. You two were going at it over her curfew."

Ashley placed her hands on her hips and nodded. "I was seventeen years old. I wanted to stay out till midnight. It didn't seem so ridiculous."

She didn't realize what she had said, what she had *remembered,* until dead silence filled the kitchen.

Jarrett stood up, knocking over his kitchen chair in his haste. Gray stared at her. Kathryn pressed a hand to her mouth.

Ashley felt the breath leave her body as she sagged back against the kitchen cabinets. "Oh, my God," she whispered. "I remember that night, that argument with Gray."

Jarrett crossed the kitchen in two long strides and gathered Ashley close. Low against her ear, he whispered, "It's coming back. I knew it would. It's all coming back. And you're going to be okay."

For the first time, she allowed herself to believe it could happen, that she could be whole again. While she gloried in the feeling, she also relished being in Jarrett's arms. More than her memory, the strength of his embrace was what felt so incredibly, totally right.

The sensation made her so giddy she could ignore the waves of disapproval that marred Gray's happiness over her memory. To hell with Gray and his overbearing manner. So what if he didn't trust Jarrett. She did. Until he gave her a reason not to trust him, she was going to go with her instincts.

"Freedom is an entire day away from my big brother." Ashley regretted the words the moment they escaped her lips. She sent a sheepish smile toward Jarrett, who walked beside her down a street in Amarillo. "That sounds really ungrateful."

"Not really. I know the guy, remember."

Sighing, she turned to peruse a table of books outside a storefront on one of the city's oldest avenues. Last night, she and Jarrett had ended up skipping the drive, but had spent today together. It had been wonderful. In the wake of last night's rain, clearer and cooler air dominated, perfect weather for a drive south to Palo Duro Canyon.

The majestic chasm, with soaring multicolored stone walls and rock formations, was an awesome sight. Lunch was a quick sandwich at a trading post named for legendary rancher Charles Goodnight, the first rancher in the West Texas Panhandle in the 1800s. The raw beauty and history of this land came alive for Ashley when viewed with Jarrett at her side.

Back in Amarillo, he had suggested a leisurely stroll through the Old San Jacinto section of town.

Several pleasant hours passed as they explored a group of quaint shops featuring antiques, collectibles and Texas memorabilia.

Not once had Jarrett asked her if she was remembering anything. Not once had she caught him studying her with the worried frowns so often on the faces of her family. Even after last night's mini-revelation, which had been followed by more blank spaces, Jarrett didn't seem to expect the dam in her brain to burst.

She appreciated his patience. Perhaps because it was in such sharp contrast to the pressure she felt at home. She sighed, weary of thinking about her brother, of feeling she was letting him down.

Deliberately, she pushed that concern out of her head and smiled at Jarrett. He was haggling with a street vendor over the price of a lace fan she had admired. He looked over at her, grinned and winked as he shaved a quarter from the price.

Ashley laughed. Though she had feared awkward fallout from last night's kiss, Jarrett had soon put her at ease. Any heightened awareness was of her own making. She admitted to herself that she liked the way his arm lingered around her waist as they walked through town. She loved the husky silk of his voice. His clean male scent. The ridiculous length of his eyelashes, so at odds with the masculine planes of his face. And the way he looked at her, as if she were the only other person on earth.

She was so caught up in admiring him that she didn't notice the children bearing down from the left.

Only when two strawberry blondes threw themselves at Jarrett did she shake herself out of her deep study.

"You two seem to be having fun," a woman drawled.

Ashley turned to find Jarrett's sister, Paige, approaching. She was pushing a stroller bearing a toddler whose bright halo of hair matched her own, as well as that of the children who were roughing up Jarrett.

"Kids, stop torturing your uncle," Paige ordered, then turned back to Ashley. "I must have lost my mind, thinking of shopping with these three rascals."

Ten-year-old Rexanne rolled her eyes and said hello to Ashley. Her year-younger brother, Joe, gave a shy smile while the baby, Matt, gurgled from the stroller.

Paige's brown eyes, so like her brother's, sparkled. She looked freckle faced and tomboyish in the bright sunshine. Paige was Kathryn's best friend and a frequent visitor at home. What Ashley liked about her was her straightforward manner. She didn't treat Ashley with kid gloves as so many people did. She was easy and natural.

Jarrett gave his sister a kiss on the cheek and reached down to pick up Matt. The toddler shrieked with pleasure as his uncle hoisted him into the air and down again. "Wow. Your little bonus baby here is a chunk of lead."

Paige laughed at his description of her unexpected youngest child. "I'm glad he's the final bonus. I'm not young enough to chase after another."

"Oh, come on. Make it an even six. Another girl to round out the numbers."

Paige pretended horror at the idea of adding to her already expansive family, but Ashley wasn't fooled. Married to True Whitman, a successful rancher, Paige was also in charge of the dude-ranch operation at her family's Double M. No doubt several more children wouldn't faze her in the least.

In addition to these three youngsters, Paige had helped her husband raise twins from his first marriage. Billy was a senior at Baylor University and planned on a career in journalism. Becca, already a horse trainer of some repute, was helping her father turn his ranch into a first-class horse-breeding operation.

"Speaking of babies," Paige said, with a pointed glance at Ashley's midsection, "you are definitely blooming."

Ashley flushed and self-consciously touched her stomach. "I guess I am."

"Now don't be embarrassed. You're beautiful," Paige admonished.

"Yes, she is," Jarrett agreed. He finished settling Matt back in the stroller and looped a casual arm around Ashley's shoulders.

Paige positively beamed her approval. The direction of her thoughts couldn't have been more obvious if she had painted them on the sidewalk in ten-inch letters. She patted her brother on the cheek and hugged Ashley. "You two look good together," she pronounced, even as she was wheeling her stroller around. "Real good."

Not waiting for their reaction, she called for her two older children and marched off down the sidewalk.

Ashley didn't realize she was holding her breath until she heard Jarrett let his out.

"I'm sorry," he muttered. "Paige is not known for holding back with her opinions or for being subtle."

"I like her style."

"You always did." Taking her arm, Jarrett turned Ashley toward the parking lot where they had left his car. Just like that, he diffused the awkwardness Paige's pointed approval might have roused.

"While we're talking about not holding back," he said, "I hope you're ready for the third degree tonight at the ranch."

They were going to have dinner at the Double M, with Jarrett's father, Rex, and his housekeeper, Tillie. The older woman was a frequent visitor at Gray and Kathryn's ranch. Ashley had learned to expect Tillie to grill her about everything. The older woman seemed convinced she would eventually ask the question that would unlock Ashley's memories.

"I'm prepared," she said. If the truth were known, she would face a roomful of Tillies if it meant this day would last just a little longer.

This morning, when she announced she would be gone until late tonight, Gray had grown downright angry. And just like last night, Ashley had argued with him, something she hadn't felt comfortable in doing before now. She understood her brother didn't care for the way Jarrett had treated her in the past. But wasn't it her decision whom she saw and what she did?

To Gray, she was still a child. His zealous protection was an effort to make up for his real or imagined part in what had happened to her. And this was nothing new. From what Ashley could piece together about her life before she disappeared, Gray had never accepted that she was an adult. She suspected it was in part a reaction to his lack of confidence in her that she had made some foolish choices. She had dropped out of college. She had jumped from job to job. She had left and caused her family untold grief.

But though her choices had been questionable, the decisions had been hers. No one put a gun to her head and forced her to drive away from Jarrett and her family and end up in California.

She didn't blame Jarrett. Or Gray. Until she knew why she had ended up pregnant and alone, she could lay no blame on the unknown father of her child. Somewhere, deep inside, Ashley suspected she had made her own choices about that, as well.

Surely she had the right to make her own decisions now. She wasn't content to be cosseted and protected by her family as she waited for her memories to return. She needed some measure of independence.

As they approached Jarrett's car, she explained how guilty she felt about resenting her brother. "I owe Gray a lot. I know he raised me and Rick. I know these past few years while I've been missing have been horrible for him. And now I'm living in his house, upsetting his family's routine—''

"Ashe, they're thrilled to have you home."

"But Gray's paying for my medical care, for the food I eat, the clothes I wear."

"Your brother is a successful veterinarian. Kathryn's business is booming. It's not a struggle for them to give you a hand."

"It's not the money."

"And you won't have to depend on them forever."

"I'm going to make sure of that."

As he inserted a key in the passenger's-door lock, Jarrett shot her a quizzical glance. "You're planning something."

Strange how well he could read her. "I told Gray and Kathryn this morning that I want a job."

Jarrett looked almost as stunned as Gray had.

She held up her hand to stave off what she thought he was going to say. "I know all the arguments. I'm a pregnant amnesiac who can't do anything."

"Who said that?"

"Guess."

"Come on, now. I know Gray can lose his cool when he's trying to make a point about something, but I'm sure he wouldn't say anything like that to you."

She admitted she might have exaggerated Gray's critical assessment of her employment potential. "He thinks I should stay home until the baby comes."

"What does Kathryn think?"

"She said I could come to work at her boutique. Gray is furious with her."

"I can imagine."

"I'm causing problems between them."

"Wait a minute." Jarrett shook his head as if he didn't believe he had heard her correctly. "Besides my sister and her husband, Gray and Kathryn are the tightest couple I know."

"I make them argue. Gray wants to put me in a little box and store me away, safe from harm. Kathryn knows that's not what I need or want. She stands up for me. So they disagree."

"You're all simply trying to adjust to a difficult situation."

"Maybe we need to adjust in separate houses."

"You want to move?"

"After I get a job."

"How about working for Kathryn?"

"I'm not going to involve her in going against Gray's wishes."

"That's probably not a bad decision." They had settled in the car and were headed out of town when Jarrett asked, "What do you really want to do, Ashley?"

Amazed at how happy a simple question could make her, she grinned.

"What's so funny?"

"You're the only person who even bothers to ask me what I want." She wished she had a clear-cut answer. "From what I understand, I had about a dozen jobs after I dropped out of college. Mostly answering phones and data entry."

"Everybody likes a pretty girl at the front desk."

She grimaced. "You make me sound like an empty-headed blonde."

Jarrett's denial was swift. "You were and are highly intelligent. You were always good with people. Outgoing. Genuinely interested. Those qualities are still inside you. How else have you managed to get through this past month, when everyone is a stranger?"

"But I was also restless—otherwise I might have worked at a job for more than six months. And now I can't remember my past, and I have a child due in about five months. Hmm..." She had to laugh. "I really sound like someone lots of people will be standing in line to hire."

Jarrett merely looked thoughtful.

Turning her bracelet around and around on her wrist, she gazed out the window. "Maybe Gray's right. Getting a job is a crazy, impossible idea."

Several miles slipped past with only the steady twin hums of the air conditioner and the tires filling the car.

Jarrett's mind was humming, as well. He didn't want to admit part of him agreed with Gray. The thought of Ashley, heavy with child, working in some office or store, raised every protective instinct inside him. At the same time, she wanted to get away. This was his chance to intercede, to take control of this situation and do something concrete. He had the means to make her happy, even as he protected her and her child.

"I have an idea, Ashe."

"Stop being an idiot and accept my fate?"

He glanced from the road to her and back again, his hands tightening on the steering wheel.

"Well?" she prompted.

He took a breath. "You could come to Dallas. You could work for me."

Chapter Five

Dallas. The very word rang with promise for Ashley.

Miles from her family's well-intentioned but stifling pressure. Miles from the frustration of memories she couldn't recall.

Dallas. With Jarrett.

A temporary opening existed in his office for someone to set his appointments, manage referrals and organize his surgery schedule. The woman who usually held the job needed some time off to care for an ill parent. Because the position was for an indefinite period of time, Ashley needn't worry about making a commitment and then needing time off for the baby. If it worked out that she wanted to stay in the city and find a job after the baby was born, Jarrett would give her a hand.

As for a place to live, Jarrett had suggested Ashley stay with him, at least for a while.

Throughout the remainder of the drive to the McMullen ranch, Ashley worried, silently and aloud, about the reasons Jarrett was making this offer. He insisted he wouldn't offer her a job that didn't exist and that he didn't mind a roommate for a while.

The thought of Jarrett as a roommate gave Ashley pause. She kept thinking of the kiss they had shared. Of how he seemed to have put it out of his mind. Of how easily he had appeared to ignore Paige lumping them together as a couple. Ashley feared she wasn't nearly as casual about both matters. And she had no business thinking of Jarrett as more than an old friend.

Yet was the danger of Jarrett's appeal worse than remaining here?

Ashley imagined months of striving for memories and failing. Of enduring her family's disappointment and worry on a daily basis. Of explaining her every move to Gray. The idea made her want to scream.

"I want to go to Dallas," she told Jarrett as he pulled to a stop at the ranch. "I want that job you're offering."

He seemed pleased. Maybe even a little triumphant. Ashley wasn't certain what it was in this latter reaction that bothered her.

As morning dawned the next day, Ashley wondered if Jarrett was still pleased with his offer and her decision. His father and Tillie were not pleased. Ashley suspected they held back the brunt of their disapproval in deference to her. No telling what they said once Jarrett brought her home and returned to the Double M. Of course, maybe they respected that Jarrett was an adult and kept the worst of their opinions to themselves.

Her family did not hold back. Against Jarrett's strenuous objections, Ashley had insisted on telling them by herself. Gray's explosion was predictable. Even Kathryn, though willing to listen, had some doubts about Ashley moving so far away with a baby due in less than five months.

Finally, Ashley grew tired of arguing and retreated to her room. Kathryn soon followed, to talk in private, to ask if Jarrett giving Ashley a job and a place to stay wasn't trading one cage for another. Wasn't Ashley simply swapping Gray's interference in her life for the dictates of another strong, forceful man—Jarrett? Was this move what Ashley wanted? Or what Jarrett wanted her to do?

Her sister-in-law's questions gave full voice to fears Ashley had not wanted to face when Jarrett made his offer. Fears she didn't want to face the next morning, either.

Because she wanted some quiet time to think things through, Ashley arose, dressed and went out before anyone else appeared.

Walking through the clear October air toward the barn, she reviewed all the objections to her move from both her brother and his wife. Gray thought she was too emotionally fragile to take on a job and manage her life without her family's help, especially with a baby on the way. He had stopped just short of calling her unstable.

Ashley had tried explaining that she wasn't cutting her family out of her life, that she simply needed some independence. For help, she would have Jarrett. Gray had asked how moving in with Jarrett represented independence in any form or fashion.

She didn't discount the validity of his question, even though she couldn't clarify, even to herself, why she felt more at home with Jarrett than with her own family.

Gray would object to her moving even if Jarrett weren't involved. Jarrett's presence was simply fat on the fire. Gray had predicted he would hurt her again.

Kathryn's questions about allowing Jarrett so much control over her life were more disturbing. Was Ashley prepared for Jarrett to have such power? To be her boss, as well as her roommate?

Ashley admitted this arrangement could be an emotional minefield. But she always came back to the same question. Was the alternative of staying here any better?

In Dallas, it would be her minefield and her emotions. *Her* life.

Brow furrowed, she went into the barn, where four horses nickered greetings. Ashley gave them feed, freshened their water and prepared to groom them. Gray would protest that these were Whitney and

Lily's chores, but Ashley liked being with the animals and making herself useful. She wanted to be busy. Once her baby was born, she would have her hands full. If she wasn't productive, she feared she would go as crazy as Gray apparently thought she already was. That's why she needed a job. A change. Something to think about besides the unanswerable questions of her past.

She ran a curry brush across the soft ebony coat of Lily's mare, Sweetie-Pie. "I have to go," she murmured. Sweetie looked at her with big, reassuring eyes.

"Remember, this horse agrees with anyone who strokes her."

Ashley turned to find her younger brother in the stall doorway, his devoted but aging beagle, Winks, at his side. Though Rick smiled, his blue-eyed gaze, so like Gray's, was serious.

She sighed. "I guess I know what's brought you up from Lubbock so early."

"Gray called last night. I couldn't sleep, so I hit the road about five."

"You've come to convince me not to move to Dallas."

"Nope." Rick stepped into the stall. In rumpled jeans and a knit shirt, his blond hair flopping over his forehead, he looked very young.

"You want me to move?"

He took the curry brush out of her hand and took over grooming Sweetie. "I don't think I would say

I *want* you to go. But I know you need to. You're not happy here."

"Gray says I won't be happy there, either."

"But you'll be with Jarrett."

Instead of answering, she knelt to scratch Winks behind his ears. She wanted to be very clear with what she said next. "Jarrett isn't the reason I want to go."

"Not the only reason, maybe."

She glanced up and caught Rick's sly grin. Sheepishly, she admitted, "All right, being with him does sound good to me."

"It always did."

The insinuation in his tone made her flush. "It's not like that between us."

"Not yet."

"Probably not ever again."

"Then you'd be defying some fundamental law of biology."

She rose to her feet. "All right, Short Stuff—" As the nickname slipped out, her hand flew to her mouth. "Oh, my. Why did I call you that?"

Rick beamed. "That's what you called me until I hit twelve, grew five inches and made you the shortest in the family."

"It just slipped out. I don't know why."

A week ago, Rick would have jumped on that memory and pumped her for more. Now, he just smiled. "It's all coming back, Ashley. All of it." Sobering, his gaze flickered to her stomach before he turned back to Sweetie.

She found she was able to be honest with him. "You and Gray are really afraid of what I'll remember."

His back to her, he applied himself to the grooming with renewed vigor. "We don't want you to relive anything terrible."

"I don't think I'll get to pick and choose what I remember."

"That's why you should be with Jarrett when it all comes back to you. You feel more comfortable with him than with us."

The hurt in Rick's voice caused Ashley a pang of remorse. "It's not that I don't want to be with you."

"You can't help the way you feel. It's not like you're deliberately cutting us out." His quick smile reassured her.

"I wish Gray would try to understand, too."

Rick shrugged. "Gray always thinks he knows best. Comes from having to make all the decisions for us for so long. He's really a good guy, you know."

"And some of his best qualities—the caring, the dedication and the protectiveness—are what drive me nuts."

Rick concentrated on the mare's already silky mane. "Before you left for California, you and Gray were fighting just the way you are now. You wanted to go off and be your own person, but he thought you should stick close by."

"Sounds like I've been searching for my true identity for longer than I've had amnesia."

"Yeah, but the trouble started when Jarrett called off your wedding for the second time."

"Jarrett isn't responsible for what happened to me. I am. Neither you nor Gray should blame him, either."

"Gray blames Jarrett only as much as he blames himself and vice versa. When you first disappeared, it was like a contest between them—who could feel more guilty."

Jarrett's blaming himself for her problems bothered Ashley. Was it guilt that had prompted this idea about Dallas? Guilt wasn't a healthy motivation. Her mind might be broken, but she understood that fundamental fact. Aloud, she wondered, "Is moving to Dallas really the right thing to do?"

"The only one who can make that decision is you," Rick replied. "This is your life, Ashe."

His acknowledgment that her fate should rest in her own hands was sweetly affirming. She hugged him. "It means everything that you believe I can make this decision on my own."

He drew away. "You have to promise to call me a lot. And you have to come home as much as you can. Otherwise, Gray will go nuts and drag you back." Rick rolled his eyes. "That's way too much conflict for me to handle while I'm still adjusting to college."

"I'll visit. I promise."

Hesitantly, as if he wasn't sure if he should, Rick placed his hand on her stomach. "When this little guy comes, I want to be there."

She cupped her hand over his. "Of course."

"We're going to love him, you know. Just like we love Lily and Whitney."

Until that moment, Ashley realized she hadn't verbalized her fear about how her fatherless child would fit in with the family. She was touched that Rick was able to reassure her unspoken fear. All along, Kathryn and Jarrett had been telling her she had a special bond with her younger brother. She was finally beginning to feel they were right.

Too moved to speak, she ruffled Rick's hair.

He looked pleased as he gestured toward the door. "Come on. Let's go talk to Gray."

"Listen to Gray is more like it."

"Just nod a lot and then do as you please. That's how I handle him." Rick laid a hand on her shoulder. "I'll be right here beside you."

Feeling adequately girded for battle, she led the way to the house, where Gray was no doubt marshaling his own forces.

In the end, they let her go without even a final, ugly stand.

Ashley called Jarrett around noon on Sunday to say she would accompany him back to Dallas. While she didn't detail the battle Jarrett was sure had ensued, she said Rick was actually happy and excited for her, Kathryn was helping her pack and Gray was staying out of the way.

When Jarrett arrived to pick up Ashley a few hours later, everyone was calm. Gray and Kathryn looked concerned and disapproving, as had Jarrett's father and Tillie, but they weren't fighting Ashley any longer. Jarrett was relieved, because he had resolved to prove to everyone that he could help Ashley through this difficult time in her life.

"You can always come home." Gray hugged Ashley, but his gaze was on Jarrett.

She said goodbye to Kathryn, Rick and the girls while Gray came over to Jarrett. His voice was low, but his threat was direct. "You'd better not hurt her."

Unwilling to be drawn into another skirmish, Jarrett put out his hand. "I won't." He felt magnanimous, as if he had won.

Though he looked doubtful, Gray shook his hand. Final goodbyes were said. Three hours later, Jarrett and Ashley were landing at the Dallas–Fort Worth Regional Airport. Lights were just piercing the autumn dusk in the metropolitan sprawl. Jarrett turned his Jeep Cherokee onto the freeway just in time to merge with the worst of the traffic from nearby Texas Stadium, where the Cowboys had just played a football game.

Ashley was full of questions, twisting this way and that as Jarrett pointed out buildings and points of interest. After nearly half an hour of bumper-to-bumper inching along the highway, he took an exit and a shortcut to the condominium he had recently purchased in the Las Colinas Complex in the Dallas suburb of Irving. Jarrett had chosen the area mainly for the convenience to his office and hospitals. The bonus was the well-orchestrated village of shops and restaurants, many of which lay along the Mandalay Canal Walk with its Venetian-built water taxis. At Las Colinas, he felt he had the best of the cosmopolitan city combined with a small-town atmosphere.

His third-floor condo was simple in comparison to some of the designer-decorated spreads of his neighbors, but was a definite step up from the dives of his medical-school and internship days. The front door opened to a foyer overlooking a cathedral-ceilinged living room. A wall of windows revealed a distant view of Lake Carolyn and the Dallas skyline. The kitchen and dining area were tucked to the left side, the guest room and bath on the other. Stairs to the right led to the master suite.

Jarrett set his small bag and Ashley's suitcase down on the tiled foyer floor and turned to her with a smile. "This is home. What do you think?"

"It's a wonderful room." Ashley paused, biting her lip. "It's very...white."

Hardly high praise, but exactly the sort of honest assessment he would have expected from the Ashley of old. Laughing, he closed the door behind them. "I just moved in a couple of months ago. Haven't had much time for decorating."

"It does look a little unfinished." Still clutching her overnight bag, Ashley moved down the shallow steps to the living area. Her fingers trailed along the back of one of the two creamy leather sofas grouped in front of the big-screen television. She adjusted a chrome-and-glass candlestick on a table, then tipped her head back to study the boldly splashed print hung over the fireplace. She frowned. ''This painting doesn't look like you.''

Jarrett had purchased the print on the same frenzied night of shopping when he had furnished the whole room. ''It was hanging with the furniture in the showroom. I told the clerk I wanted everything, from the print to the lamps.''

''I guess that explains these,'' Ashley murmured, touching the burgundy shade of a twisted-iron-and-chrome lamp.

Forestalling further criticism, Jarrett crossed the room and opened the door to the guest room. ''I think you'll like this better. The furniture came from the ranch. And a wo—'' He caught himself and cleared his throat. ''A friend put the colors and stuff together in this room.''

The warm maple furniture and sunny yellow decor of the guest room met with approval from Ashley. If she had noticed Jarrett's fumbling over the decorating explanation, she gave no sign. He supposed there was no reason not to tell her that a woman he had dated briefly had picked out the comforter and curtains in the bedroom and the rugs and towels in the adjoining bath. But there was also no reason to rush into those sort of details, either. That woman was gone from his life, while Ashley was here.

She was here in his home with him. He had a chance to make up for some of the harm he had once done her. He had a responsibility, a duty to help her.

Jarrett was determined not to screw this up. He

owed Ashley. She needed him. That's why he had made this offer. She felt comfortable with him in a way she didn't with anyone else. He could help her regain her memory and deal with her coming child. He could protect them both.

Surely, he could ignore how pretty she looked in the soft light of the bedside lamps. How her skin glowed. How her loose cotton knit shirt managed to accentuate rather than hide the ripening curves of her body. She set her overnight bag on the bed, turning so that her breasts were silhouetted against the light. Jarrett wondered if her lush breasts would look or feel different from the way he remembered. Fuller, maybe. The nipples darker, probably. Changing in preparation for the child she carried.

The thought of Ashley with a baby cradled to her breast was suddenly, inexplicably erotic. Jarrett's sex hardened in response. Immobilized by the sudden tide of desire, he was aware of Ashley speaking to him, though he honestly couldn't focus on what she was saying.

She regarded him with a puzzled frown. ''Is something wrong?''

Just this incredible arousal that came simply from looking at you. He swallowed those unspoken words with a groan he tried to disguise with a cough.

''Jarrett?''

''I'm fine,'' he assured her gruffly, ashamed of his traitorous thoughts. ''I'll get your suitcase, and you can settle in.'' Though he worried about his ability to walk, he turned toward the foyer.

Once her luggage was deposited in her room, he saw to putting his own things away upstairs and ordered a pizza for dinner. He managed to enjoy Canadian bacon with extra cheese and sundried tomatoes while sitting with Ashley in front of the TV without his libido launching into overdrive.

She was quiet, tucked into the opposite corner of the sofa where he sat. She studied the room and barely paid attention to the television program featuring paranormal-investigating FBI agents.

Finally, Jarrett hit the mute button on the remote control. "You okay, Ashe?"

She sighed, her expression sheepish. "I'm sitting here, wondering how I can know I hate the decor of this room when I don't know so many other, more important things about myself."

"A person knows what they respond to, what colors please them, what makes them laugh or cry. Those feelings are innate, not necessarily linked to a memory."

She curled her legs under her. "Tell me about me, Jarrett."

The command surprised him. "What do you mean?"

"Everyone else has been pretty vocal about what I used to be like. My family has focused in on little things, like what flavor ice cream I liked or the books I used to read to Rick at bedtime or the names of the pets we raised. They've told me about vacations and holidays, good times and bad. You've told me about places we went. Things we did with friends. Now tell me something important. Something only you could know.''

He could detail 1001 beautiful, intimate secrets they had shared. But that wasn't smart. Not when he knew how easily he could forget the role he needed to play in her life now.

"Tell me about the first time we met," she suggested. "What did I say? How did I look?"

"You looked like an angel." The words slipped out before he thought.

Ashley leaned her cheek against the back of the couch, looking shyly, sweetly pleased, though she protested, "That doesn't really tell me anything."

Grinning, he drew one leg up on the couch as he faced her. "Okay...let me see. We met at a dance."

"At school?"

"Are you kidding? I was a college man, and you were a senior in high school. This was at a street dance in Amarillo. It was about this time of year, and you and Gray and Rick had only been in town a couple of months. I was home for the weekend, bored and looking for trouble."

She chuckled. "I would have thought pre-med students would be too busy for trouble."

"I was a wild one in those days."

"Was I wild, too?"

"I wanted you to be."

The laugh they shared was soft and perilously intimate. Jarrett looked away with reluctance and continued his story. "Anyway...the night we met, you were with some girls from your class. I think they dared you to ask me to dance.''

She laughed. "So I approached you first."

"Only because you beat me to the punch. I was headed your way." He rubbed a hand across his jaw, remembering. "I saw you first thing that night. You had on this white, frilly-looking blouse and these tight, tight blue jeans tucked into boots. You looked damn good."

"Pure animal lust, huh?"

Feeling some uncomfortable stirrings of just such an emotion, Jarrett nodded.

"What did we do?"

"We danced. Every dance for the rest of the night."

She gave him a long, considering glance. "I wouldn't have taken you for such a dancer."

"I just liked holding you."

His husky admission seemed to make Ashley uncomfortable. She looked away. "Did you take me home?"

"About an hour late for your curfew." He laughed softly. "As you can imagine, that got me off to a real fine start with Gray. That's what led to the argument you had the next night, when I came to pick you up for our first official date."

"So we saw a lot of each other after that."

"I came home from Tech as often as I could. You and some of your friends would come down to visit some weekends, as well. Gray thought you were checking out the campus."

Ashley had a feeling about what she had really been checking out. She could imagine a younger Jarrett, as tall and dark and devastatingly attractive as he was now, but with a wild edge that maturity had polished to a subtle sheen. What girl could have resisted him? For that matter, what woman could resist him now?

That question caused her breath to catch. The room was suddenly silent. Jarrett's dark-eyed gaze moved over her, as tangible as a caress. He looked at her with memories heavy on his mind; she returned his glance with an attraction born in the moment. Forcibly, she reminded herself of the distance that lay between then and now.

She broke the spell and swung her feet to the floor. "I should turn in early. Big day tomorrow."

"Big day today. Maybe you ought to stay here tomorrow, get settled in. I don't have surgery scheduled tomorrow, but I do have to see some patients at the hospital before my appointments begin at the office."

"Do you need to clear hiring me with someone at the office?"

His grin said she was right on the money. "I know everything's going to be fine, but it might be a good idea if I brought you in to meet everyone tomorrow afternoon."

She felt a pinprick of concern. "Jarrett, are you sure you haven't invented this job for me?"

"I wouldn't insult you with a made-up job," Jarrett assured her, as he had done yesterday,

She had no choice but to believe him.

She got to her feet and started toward her bedroom. Jarrett rose, as well, and was watching her when she turned in the doorway to offer a last goodnight.

"I hope you have everything you need," he said.

"Everything but a new wardrobe," she quipped. "Most of the clothes I bought when I first came home don't fit. I've got mainly your sister's castoffs for maternity wear."

"We'll go shopping tomorrow. I'll get you anything you need."

Her spine stiffened. "You're not buying me clothes, as well as giving me a home and a job."

"Consider it a loan."

"No," she said. "We're not going to start that."

His jaw set in a stubborn line. "And we're not going to start nitpicking things to death, either. Worrying over a few dollars here or there is stupid."

She resented the implication in his words, that her concerns and desires were stupid. "I'm not your personal charity case."

He looked well and truly angry. "That's an insulting thing to say to me. To someone who cares about you."

Ashley started a retort, then bit her lip. This was their first night. She didn't want to start off by arguing. Tomorrow and the day after and from here on out, she would simply refuse to allow Jarrett to do her more favors than were absolutely necessary. The whole point of coming here was to stand on her own two feet. To lean on him only as much as she absolutely had to.

"I'm too tired to argue right now," she told him. "I'm going to turn in."

He took a deep breath and nodded, evidently deciding to let this argument go, as well. "Good night, Ashe."

Was it her imagination, or did his voice deepen perceptibly on her name? Ashley closed the door before allowing her gaze to meet his again. She didn't know if she was afraid of what she might find in his expression or of how she might react.

Safely inside her room, she leaned back against the door and sighed. She didn't want her emotions to be caught in the undercurrents that flashed between the two of them. She had enough problems without becoming entangled in sexual attraction.

She was here because Jarrett offered her freedom with a healthy dose of security.

Yet she couldn't stop thinking about Jarrett's hands. Broad palmed. Long fingered. Obviously strong. No doubt skillful, considering his profession. Those hands could stitch together torn flesh. He could repair and reinvent. She imagined his touch could be both gentle and insistent. As potent as that unexpected kiss they had shared Friday night. That delicious, all-consuming kiss...

Her baby moved with fluttering, soft motions, and Ashley crashed from daydreams to reality. With another sigh, she pushed away from the door and moved toward the bathroom to get ready for bed. In the mirror over the dresser, she caught a glimpse of herself—hair messy, face shiny, her oversize top accentuating rather than disguising her thickening body. What a joke for her to imagine Jarrett might be looking at her with interest, that Friday's kiss had been anything other than an impulse founded on the past she didn't recall.

What she had to do was set foolishness aside and think of him as her boss. And her roommate. Jarrett was just an old friend who was giving her a job and a place to live. He was just a guy.

Her casual attitude was easy to maintain in private. Early the next morning, however, Ashley walked in the kitchen and found a sleepy, tousle-haired Jarrett, clad only in a pair of boxers, waiting for his coffee to brew. He was yawning, stretching and rubbing a hand over his face, so he didn't see her at first. All her good intentions crashed and burned.

She had more than enough time to peruse his washboard abs, his muscular arms and the dark hair that angled from the center of his broad chest to a point somewhere beneath the boxers that clung perilously low on his narrow hips. Nothing about this man was "just" anything. He was simply superb.

He saw her and jumped.

She flushed and drew the edges of her thin robe together.

The coffee gurgled into the pot, a stream of heated liquid that had nothing on the awareness that jumped between them.

Chapter Six

"Ashe? You ready to go?"

Jarrett's voice calling from the living room startled Ashley. He was home, ready to take her to the office.

"Coming," she called, and gave her outfit one last adjustment. She wasn't sure what she dreaded most—crossing the hurdles that awaited at Jarrett's office or just facing him again.

This morning, after clumsily fleeing the kitchen, she had remained in her bedroom while he left for early rounds at the hospital and appointments at the office. He had called before noon, to tell her everything was set with her job and he was coming to pick her up. That's when nerves had hit her in earnest.

She had spent the past half hour trying on the

clothes she had brought with her, finally settling on a kelly green knit dress, a navy jacket and a brightly colored scarf. The outfit was an amalgamation of clothes given to her by Paige and Kathryn. Nothing, save the scarf, seemed to suit her.

But they were all she had, so she took a deep breath and went out to greet Jarrett. His conservative gray suit was every bit as appealing as the boxers she had caught him in this morning. The memory made her flush.

He was at ease, apparently unaffected by their early-morning, half-dressed encounter. Hopefully, he had been too sleepy to notice what a gauche idiot she had made of herself. His dark eyes warmed with appreciation as they scanned her from head to toe. "You look terrific."

"Do I?" She brushed an uncertain hand through her hair. She was happy with the new style Kathryn's hairdresser had given her last week. That, at least, felt like her own choice.

Jarrett gestured toward the door. "Come on. Greta's excited to meet you."

Once they were in the car and headed toward his office, Ashley quizzed him about the people she was going to meet. "Greta's the office manager, right?"

Busy merging into traffic, Jarrett nodded. "I think of her as the office lieutenant. She keeps things running like a top."

"She sounds very efficient."

He shot her an encouraging smile. "She's also one of the kindest, sweetest people I've ever known. She lives here in Las Colinas, not far from my place, and she'll be giving you a ride most mornings, since I'm usually at the hospital long before it's time for you to be at the office.''

Ashley bit her lip. ''I hate to put her out like that.''

''She suggested it.''

The city scenery flashed by the window for a few minutes before Ashley spoke. ''Did you tell Greta all about me?''

''Your memory?''

''And the baby.''

''I thought I should.'' His eyebrows drew together as he glanced at her. ''Is that okay with you?''

''Of course.''

''She thought your memory loss was something we shouldn't make a big deal about around the office. Gossip, you know. People can blow it all out of proportion.''

That made Ashley chuckle. ''Good Lord, how much bigger can it get than total amnesia?''

He laughed, as well. ''You're right, I guess. But I didn't think you'd want to be answering all kinds of questions. There are a few people who know I had a friend who was missing. They might put two and two together, but then again, they might not. Especially since we've been able to keep all this out of the media.''

The phalanx of family and friends who had surrounded Ashley since she came home had done a good job of keeping her story private. ''I'm really glad I didn't end up as a feature on the evening news.

There will be enough questions when it's obvious to everyone that I'm pregnant, and there's no father.''

"That's no one's business but yours." Jarrett pulled into the garage beside a large medical complex and brought his Cherokee to a stop in a parking space that bore his name.

Ashley's palms began to perspire.

As if he knew how her nerves were jumping, Jarrett reached over and squeezed her forearm in reassurance. "I wouldn't have suggested you do this if I didn't think you could."

"I'm not sure why you have so much faith in me."

"Because I know you better than you know yourself."

"That's no great accomplishment," she retorted with a wry smile.

"So trust me."

Trusting him was alarmingly easy, as it had been ever since he walked into her upended life.

His hand slipped down to cover hers. "Let's go meet Greta."

Greta Layton was not the grandmotherly, gray-haired matron Ashley had imagined on the basis of what Jarrett had told her. She was a redhead, probably in her late forties, tall and slim, with a killer smile, twinkling green eyes behind rhinestone-studded glasses and a slow Texas drawl. She wore a chartreuse smock over fuchsia leggings, a combination that echoed the colors in her small, plant-filled office.

"My God, but you're pretty," she said when Jarrett presented Ashley to her.

Unsure whether that was an asset or a liability, Ashley just smiled.

Rising from behind her desk, Greta tsk-tsked. "Dr. Mac, every female client you have will ask to be remade to look like this honey child."

"Natural beauty can never be duplicated," Jarrett retorted.

"Shh, now." Greta lifted an elaborately manicured finger to her lips. "Don't be saying that too loud. People come here looking for miracles. And it would take one to create skin like this creature has."

Feeling like a bug under a microscope, Ashley cleared her throat. "Y'all are embarrassing me."

"Sorry about that." Greta extended her hand. "I just didn't expect Dr. Mac's old friend from back home to be a stunner."

"All I am is grateful," Ashley replied. "I appreciate Jarrett arranging for me to take over this job for the next few months, and I'm grateful to you for giving me a chance."

"You're doing us a favor. I hate like the dickens dealing with those temporary agencies, which was what we were going to have to do." The older woman waved Jarrett toward the hallway. "Dr. Mac, I think you've got a full slate of appointments this afternoon. Leave Ashley to me."

Jarrett disappeared, and Ashley was soon caught up in a whirlwind of activity. Her jacket was disposed of, and she donned a purple smock. All the office personnel were similarly adorned in bright colors. "We like things cheerful around here," Greta explained.

Then there were forms to be completed for her employment, a tour of the large, ultramodern offices, introductions to doctors, nurses and office staff. Ashley spent the last several hours of the day with the woman whose job she was taking over.

Her assigned space was a cubbyhole in a maze of other, similar squares in the inner office, near Jarrett's office and a group of examination rooms. His administrative assistant explained that office appointments and surgery schedules were tracked by computer. Ashley discovered, to her great relief, that this was a simple enough task. More complicated was the time she would spend on the telephone with hospitals, making arrangements for tests or operating rooms. The medical terms were unfamiliar and would take some study. In addition, Ashley would be expected to pull the files on incoming patients, have them ready for each appointment, then refile them afterward.

Ashley had been worried that the office skills she had acquired before her memory loss would have deserted her. But after two hours of observing and helping the woman she was replacing, she thought the most difficult part of her job would be getting used to everyone calling Jarrett "Dr. Mac."

She tried not to worry about the speculative looks some of the other employees gave her. She could imagine what they were thinking—that she had this job because of her relationship with Jarrett, not because of her abilities. Of course, they were right. That made Ashley determined to show them all how hard she could work.

Jarrett's administrative assistant departed late in the day. Ashley was working on some files when Jarrett paused at her cubbyhole's counter to report he was headed to the hospital to check on a patient.

Greta, who had come back to see how Ashley's day had progressed, offered to give her a ride home.

He shook his head. "I'll be back in less than an hour. I was planning on taking Ashley out for dinner to celebrate her first day on the job."

"Jarrett, that's not necessary," Ashley objected. She noted the glance given them by a passing nurse who had obviously overheard the comment.

But he insisted and left with a grin and a wave.

Greta gave Ashley a thoughtful look. She leaned forward and lowered her voice. "Please don't worry what anyone around here thinks about your getting this job."

Ashley tried to pretend unconcern. Greta was too sharp to buy that, however.

"It doesn't matter why you were hired," the redhead advised. "It's how you do the work that matters." She left Ashley with a final, encouraging smile.

Sighing with weariness, Ashley sat back in her chair. In the office around her, activity was winding down. Several people called friendly goodbyes as they passed. She responded in kind, then slipped her shoes off her aching feet. If this afternoon's pace was any indication, she was getting her wish about staying busy.

She passed the time waiting for Jarrett by going through the appointment program once again. She was massaging her toes and yawning when he finally startled her by appearing on the other side of the counter.

"I had almost given up on you."

"I'm sorry." His words were belied by the wide grin that split his face. "I got caught up with one of my patients, a burn victim whose first skin graft was Friday morning."

"Any complications?"

"She looks good so far, but she was pretty angry that I left her to another doctor's care all weekend and most of today. I had to do some groveling before coming back here." He went on to explain that a house fire had devastated the girl's family, leaving two brothers dead.

"And the parents?"

"The father was at work. The mother got Megan out, but couldn't reach her two sons."

Hand fluttering automatically to her stomach, Ashley tried to imagine such a horrible event. "I feel for them all."

"This family has a spirit that won't quit. Especially little Megan."

Ashley settled back in her chair. "One day here, and already I'm amazed at what all of you do." She ticked off a list of procedures she had heard discussed—everything from breast reconstruction for a cancer survivor to the complete rebuilding of an accident victim's face. "I thought I'd be dealing only with people having nose jobs and face-lifts."

"I do those, too."

"But there's a lot more to your practice than I dreamed. Look at this little girl you're helping. You're probably rescuing her from a life of pain, mental and physical."

He waved off her praise. "Don't go melodramatic on me, Ashley. I'm no savior. I love what I do, and try to do it well." He smoothly changed the subject, focusing on her. "How was your day? It looked to me as if they already had you hard at work."

"Everyone has been very nice. I feel reasonably confident that in a day or so, I can handle most of this."

"I never doubted that."

She flashed him a smile, but groaned when she attempted to slide her aching feet back into her navy pumps. "Oh, man, tomorrow I'm wearing comfortable shoes."

"Does that mean we need to skip dinner and go shopping?"

"Greta and I have made a date for the mall this weekend. I'll get by until then."

"So let's go eat."

"From the looks of what I saw in your refrigerator this morning, I think we ought to hit the grocery store, too."

"Coffee and week-old Chinese food doesn't do much for you, huh?"

"The only edible thing I could find for breakfast and lunch was left-over pizza."

He was shamefaced. "Jeez, I went off and left you this morning without thinking about food. You must be starving, and that can't be good for the baby."

His concern was almost comical. She bore his solicitous behavior gracefully during dinner at a nearby steakhouse. But when they reached the grocery store, and he had asked her for the fourth time whether she was too tired for shopping, she put an end to his guilt trip. "Cut it out or I'm going to wish I had stayed in Amarillo with Gray. I'm fine. Completely fine."

Jarrett flushed and went on the defensive. "Don't get mad. I just don't want you to overdo it."

"I can decide whether or not I'm overdoing."

"But the baby—"

"Is just fine. As I am. I'm pregnant, not terminally ill."

This last comment drew chuckles from several nearby shoppers. An older man patted Jarrett on the shoulder. "Humor her, son. Little women need pampering when they're having our babies."

Ashley fumed at the "little women" crack, while Jarrett grinned. He didn't bother correcting the man about the child she was carrying being his.

She imagined everyone assumed, quite naturally, that they were a couple. Just two domestic partners, shopping for toilet paper and frozen peas, bickering good-naturedly over orange juice with or without the pulp. The situation felt too good, too right, and she needed to put the brakes on before she got too comfortable.

As soon as they arrived home and put the groceries away, she said she was going to bed.

"We could watch a movie or something," Jarrett suggested. "Pop some corn."

"I'm tired," she said, even though nothing appealed to her more than settling down in front of the tube with Jarrett. She just couldn't give in to that impulse. Spending every spare moment with him would be the start of an unhealthy domestic pattern. They weren't a couple; they couldn't act like one.

Jarrett didn't argue, though he gave her a long worried look.

She retreated to the bedroom that immediately felt like a box. The temptation to go out and join Jarrett was huge. She picked up the phone and called Gray and Kathryn, then Rick. They were just ending their conversation when a knock sounded at her door.

She hung up the phone and opened the door. Jarrett had changed from his suit to jeans and an old sweatshirt. *Monday Night Football* boomed from the television in the living room behind him.

"I just wanted to see if you were really okay," he said.

"Why wouldn't I be?" she said, trying not to sound as annoyed as she felt.

"You seemed sort of...distant. I wanted to make sure you're feeling all right."

"I'm fine," she insisted. Her hand fluttered to the

tightly buttoned collar of her demure robe. Why did she feel so self-conscious? Why couldn't he just leave her alone? More important, why was she so pleased that he wasn't leaving her alone?

He shifted awkwardly from foot to foot and cleared his throat.

"Is there something else?" she asked.

"No...I guess not. Good night."

Ashley closed her door with more force than she intended.

Jarrett stood unmoving, staring hard at the door. Was this the way it was going to be? Every night, would Ashley close herself up in there alone? But if that's what she wanted, why should it bother him? He shouldn't be concerned. Just because they had been getting along like a house afire until they got home from the grocery store was no reason to feel slighted. She was tired; she didn't want to be with him. She didn't owe him the pleasure of her company. No big deal. Except that it bothered the hell out of him.

Without pausing to think, he rapped on Ashley's door. She opened it too quickly to have been in bed. He suspected she had been standing there, staring at her side of the door as hard as he had been staring at his. She was still wearing her robe, that damn prissy robe she'd had on this morning when they collided in the kitchen. A robe totally at odds with her sexy cascade of golden hair or her delicate, beautiful face. He had avoided replaying this morning's sizzling moments all day, but it came back to him now—in detail.

Frowning, he said without preamble, "I want to know if you're upset with me."

Ashley rocked back on her heels. "What?"

"You act like you're angry, and I don't know why or what I've done. I wish you'd tell me."

"Good Lord, Jarrett. There's nothing wrong."

"I just don't want to screw this up. Make you uncomfortable. Do something wrong."

She tucked a strand of hair behind one ear and sighed. "You're not doing anything wrong. Except maybe being too solicitous."

He rubbed the bristle on his jaw. "I'm sorry. I just want this to work out."

She frowned again. "The way you say that makes me think you're worried it's not going to work. Did something happen at the office? Is someone angry that you hired me?"

"Angry? Of course not." He blew out a frustrated breath. "Hell, Ashe, could you come out here and talk. I feel like I'm at some stranger's door, taking a survey."

She obliged, advancing into the room with her arms folded firmly across her midriff. "Okay, what's really wrong?"

He muted the football game. Then, hands thrust deep in his pockets, he paced in front of the television set. "I just don't want you to isolate yourself."

She murmured something under her breath. "Jarrett, I simply wanted to go to bed early. I didn't expect you to take it so personally.''

"That's not it. I just want..." What did he want, anyway? How was he going to put into words what he didn't understand himself? The fact was he could barely stand to have her out of his sight. When he extended the offer for her to move in with him, he had every intention of giving her the space she wasn't getting with her family. Now that she was here, he wanted to crowd her. Be with her. Watch over her every move.

Damn it, he hadn't counted on the attraction he felt for her growing even stronger. Despite the kiss they had shared, he had not invited her here in order to rekindle their romance. Things were too complicated to consider such a move. There was her memory loss. The baby. The man who might even now be searching for her and their child.

Jealousy knifed through Jarrett. He deserved the pain. He had lost Ashley, pushed her away. What he didn't deserve were any second chances with her.

Confusion wrinkled Ashley's brow. "Jarrett, what do you want?"

He took a deep breath. Dear God, he was being irrational. Twenty-four hours with her living here, and already all he could focus on was the door she kept closing between them. "I'm sorry," he said.

"But what's the deal with me going in my room?"

"There's no deal," he said with a sweep of his arms. "No deal whatsoever. I was being...stupid."

Ashley looked as confused as ever. "I don't want

to be a problem, Jarrett. If I'm already bugging you by being here, Gray offered to pay for an apartment until I—''

"No," he said firmly. "That's not necessary. You are absolutely not bugging me. You need to stay here. Just do whatever you want to do."

She pointed over her shoulder. "I was going to bed."

"Good. That's good." Jarrett was well aware he sounded as asinine as one of the characters on that sitcom where everyone sat around on couches at a coffee shop. Hell, he felt just like one of those characters, all twitchy and on edge. Like a bear sniffing around a honey tree, Tillie would say.

He released another long breath. "I think I'm going out for a few minutes."

Ashley nodded again.

"I want some...ice cream," he improvised.

"We bought those dairy bars tonight. They're in the freezer."

"But I want ice cream. A sundae or something." She said nothing.

Jarrett headed for the foyer. He put on his running shoes and grabbed his keys off a table. He had the door open and was about to call out a good-night when Ashley stopped him.

"Would it bother you if I came, too?"

He faced her. "You want ice cream?"

"I didn't until you mentioned it. But now..."

"Is this like a pregnancy craving or something?"

"I don't know. Maybe."

For some reason, that made him grin like an even bigger idiot than he had already proved himself to be. "There's an ice-cream shop down on the canal walk that's open until ten."

"I'll get dressed."

She was in jeans and a sweater within five minutes. They decided to walk through the cool October evening air.

Just like a dozen other couples they encountered on the way.

Just as if they did this every night.

As she savored the final bite of her hot-fudge sundae with whipped cream and nuts, Ashley realized she was doing exactly what she had sworn to avoid. She was feeling too good about being with Jarrett. Too happy. Too content.

Oh, she could lie to herself, pretend they were just two old friends out for a sundae, roomies enjoying a treat together.

But that thinking was just bull.

The man who took her arm as they strolled back to the condo wasn't a friend. He was much, much more. They had a connection that had reached past the walls in her mind and made her recognize him when she had known no one else. Their kinship was deep, too complex for her to analyze easily.

Could she call her feelings for him romantic? She was attracted to him. No doubt about that. She liked the breadth of his shoulders. His infectious grin. The mesmerizing sparkle of his dark eyes. All those admirable physical attributes were enhanced by the security she felt when they were together. Why did she trust him so completely? Because she had called his name in the hospital?

Whatever the reason, she simply loved being with him.

As her youngest niece might say, she was in deep doo-doo.

Ashley hated admitting Gray and Kathryn might have been right about the dangers of living with Jarrett. Becoming dependent on him would be the easiest thing she could do. Not because she wanted to lean on anyone. She wanted, more than anything, to stand on her own two feet. But knowing Jarrett was close by felt damn wonderful, all the same.

Could feeling this good really be wrong for her?

Her brother thought Jarrett was all wrong for her. He had predicted heartache if she let herself grow close to Jarrett again. Ashley kept searching her mind, her soul, trying to recall the feelings of disappointment and betrayal that had driven her away from home, feelings Jarrett supposedly caused. But her memories were as blank as ever.

All she knew was the way she felt right now.

For this night, and for most of the next two weeks, Ashley did her best to set aside her worries and simply follow her instincts. She tried not to obsess about how those inclinations always led her back to Jarrett.

She was busy learning her job at the office, dealing with a dizzying blur of patients and co-workers. She knew there was talk about her and Jarrett. Word had gotten out about her living with him. Ashley refused to be drawn into any deeply personal conversations or explanations. A couple of people had guessed she was pregnant, a fact it wasn't going to be easy to hide if she kept packing on the pounds. Greta was a big help, gleefully squashing gossip every chance she could.

Ashley kept her contact with Jarrett at work professional. He had surgery most mornings, and back-to-back appointments in the afternoons. She handed him files, made phone calls and constantly updated his ever changing and busy schedule.

Most nights, she made dinner. Or Jarrett brought in takeout. Often, he was called in to the hospital. She never intended to sit up and wait for him, but she just couldn't seem to sleep until she knew he was home. He chided her, but she thought he was pleased on some level, as well.

Occasionally, she wondered about all the time he gave her. He had a friend from med school he played racquetball with twice a week. He lunched with some of his partners. But he spent most of his free time with her. If there had been women in his life before Ashley returned, she saw no sign of them now.

She went shopping with Greta and blew almost all of the money she had on clothes to carry her through her pregnancy. The second weekend after her arrival, Jarrett took her to a Cowboys game. From watching televised games with him, Ashley had discovered she loved football. Jarrett said this was nothing new.

They were in the stands at the stadium when Jarrett admitted the truth to himself about what he was feeling for Ashley. She was jumping up and down, cheering a Cowboy interception, going wild with the rest of the crowd. She looked exactly like the girl she had been before she left Texas, before he broke her heart and sent her running away to God only knew what. In the cool autumn air, her cheeks were as rosy as her cherry-red sweater. Her blond hair bouncing. She was full of life and energy. Bright, shining and perfect. The mercurial beauty he had sought to hold from the moment they met.

It was more than sex, though his desire for Ashley had never abated, was unchanged even now. His craving for her was keyed to a higher level. He couldn't give it a name, didn't dare flirt with a word like *love*. That word had been tossed around between them too casually in their past. He would not go there.

He focused on the need she aroused in him. Having Ashley at his side lit up his world. She filled up a place inside him that he hadn't realized was empty.

He was awash with this realization when the Cowboys converted their turnover into a last-second, game-winning touchdown. Caught up in the excitement, Ashley threw her arms around Jarrett.

He kissed her. Without thinking or planning. In that crowded stadium, surrounded by thousands of cheering strangers, they kissed with the familiarity of old lovers. With the heat of newly discovered passion. They kissed while the crowds around them erupted in a wild victory celebration.

They kissed until Ashley pulled away, her expression stunned. "Why did you do that?"

"I couldn't *not* kiss you." Unable to stop his giddy grin, Jarrett brushed confetti and popcorn out of her hair.

Her amber eyes were very solemn. "It was crazy."

"And you loved it."

She glanced down, her eyelashes a dark sweep against her cheeks. Only the slight trembling at the corners of her mouth gave away the smile she was trying to suppress.

He tipped her face up to his once again. "Admit it, Ashe. We've been skirting around this from the moment I kissed you down by the creek at home."

"We agreed that was a mistake."

He caught her close once more, holding her tight while the crowd around them surged toward the field. "This doesn't feel like a mistake." He took her hand and drew her toward an exit. "Let's get out of here."

Chapter Seven

They battled their way through the crowds and were in the Jeep in the parking garage when Jarrett started to kiss Ashley again.

She held him off. "This isn't smart, Jarrett."

"Why not?"

"It's exactly what Gray and Kathryn said would happen if I came to Dallas with you."

"Does that make it a bad thing?"

Her brow knit. "I didn't want Gray to be right."

Jarrett took her hand. "Ashe, honey, what's happening between you and me has nothing to do with Gray. He was part of our problem in the past."

"Is he really the reason we didn't get married?"

The question made Jarrett shift uncomfortably in

his seat. There was no denying Gray's interference in their relationship, especially when they were very young. As for their final failure, however, Jarrett couldn't pin that on anyone but himself. At the same time, he didn't want Gray's opinions carrying any undue weight with the decisions Ashley might make now.

"Your whole reason for moving to Dallas was to think for yourself. Put Gray's pessimism out of your mind."

"That's all I've been doing," she said. "For two weeks, I've ignored the voice that's been rumbling in my head, telling me to pull back from you, to be careful. But now I can't help but remember what Gray told me about my relationship with you. He doesn't trust you."

"But you do."

"Yes, but..." Her gaze sought his and then faltered as she pulled her hand from his. "I guess I don't really trust myself."

"You don't feel something special is going on between us?"

"I didn't say that."

"You want me to back off? You want to forget this attraction?"

She squeezed her eyes shut. "I didn't say that, either."

He was confused. "I don't understand."

"Jarrett, please." Looking up, she touched his arm. "You're forgetting something pretty big here."

"What?"

"The baby, of course."

He was more puzzled than ever. "I haven't forgotten your child. I don't see what he or she has to do with this."

Ashley did a double take. One hand clenched against her stomach. "Are you insane? This baby has everything to do with every choice I make for the rest of my life."

Jarrett rubbed his chin. "I'm not saying the baby shouldn't be your first concern. What I don't get is why this child precludes you from finding out if we can work things out between us."

She slumped back in the seat. "Jarrett, I don't even know who I am. Unless something changes soon, I won't even be able to tell my son or my daughter who their father is. For all I know, I'm already committed to someone else. With all of that to consider, how can I even think about having a relationship with you?"

"You kissed me like a great deal of thought had gone into it."

Guilty color flooded her cheeks. "Thinking about it and doing it are two very different things."

"Going for what you want involves a big risk. Courage."

Her eyes flashed fire. "Are you implying that I'm a coward?"

"On the contrary. The way you've pulled yourself together since we found you in Canada has been damn courageous. But then, you were never a coward."

"You talk as if I should know how to behave, based on my past actions. You forget I can't remember that person. I don't know what Ashley Elizabeth Grant is supposed to do in any given situation. Most days, I'm in uncharted territory the minute I open my eyes."

Irritation roughened his voice. "I told you this once before. For some reason, your mind has blocked out names and dates and places from your past, but you are the same person you've always been. You're exactly the woman you were when you left here."

"I wasn't pregnant with another man's child then."

"That isn't important."

"How can you keep saying that?"

"Because it's true."

When she shrank back, Jarrett realized he had become too emphatic. He took a deep breath. "I'm sorry, Ashley. I didn't mean to yell at you."

Folding her arms across her middle, she stared straight ahead. People continued to stream from Texas Stadium, but they could have been alone on a deserted island. "You're not being realistic. No matter what you think, I can't pretend I was born the day I woke up in that hospital."

"What's important is what's happening now."

Her laugh was bitter. "That's easy for you to say, considering you know your past. I don't."

"But you will."

"I'm not so certain of that any longer." Her features clouded. "And it's so damn frustrating. Especially when it comes to the past we shared and the feeling I have for you now. I have only half of our story to work with. I don't know how I really felt or what I thought before I left here.''

''And maybe that's lucky for me.''

''Meaning what?''

''The slate's as clean as it can get. We've essentially started over.''

''But you're the only one who got a full set of the rules to play by.''

''This isn't a game. The only rules are the ones we make up together.'' He reached out to touch her cheek. ''I admit I have an unfair advantage. I remember how wonderful you were. I see you haven't really changed. I want to rediscover what we—what *I* let slip away.''

She tilted her head to the side, studying him with a thoughtful frown. ''Maybe I'm the one with the advantage,'' she murmured. ''You're dazzled by memories of a first love. You're not seeing me just for what I am.''

He stroked his fingers through her hair, down her jaw to her lips. ''You're wrong. I am dazzled by how you are right now. I can't wait to be with you every day. That's been the amazing part of you moving here. Every time I realize I'm coming home to you, I think I'm the luckiest guy in the world.''

She hesitated. ''Could that be because I was gone for so long and you blamed yourself?''

His denial was emphatic. ''I don't see why being

happy to see you every single day can't be just what it is. You're a beautiful, intelligent woman.''

"Who will soon be as big as a barrel with some-one else's baby.''

He laid his hand on her stomach. "I don't care. It's your baby.''

"You say that now....''

"I don't think I'll be changing my mind.''

She laughed again. "Damn, but you're convincing.''

"Bedside manner is one of my strong suits.''

"This isn't a bed.''

His mouth lowered toward hers. "The seats fold down. We could give it a go.''

He caught her chuckle beneath his lips. Slowly, with careful strokes, he parted her mouth, probing, tasting, savoring. She groaned, deep in her throat. He pulled away, grinning. "You always made that sound.''

"What sound?''

"The same one you make when you eat ice cream or good Chinese. Halfway between bliss and ecstasy.''

"Only halfway?'' she teased.

"The sound you make when you're all the way at ecstasy is much, much louder.''

She buried her head against his shoulder. "Do you know how frustrating it is that you know all these things that I don't know about myself?''

"I know about frustration,'' he said. "Frustration

is watching your bedroom door close every single night.''

''Every single night for only two weeks.'' She made a soft sound of disgust. ''You're weak.''

He cupped her face and looked into her eyes. ''You forget. It's been three years, ten months and a few odd days since you left a door open for me.''

''When was that?''

''The morning you left.''

''I'm beginning to think our relationship was more complicated than I ever dreamed.''

''I'd like to make it simple.'' He kissed her again. ''Let's go home and see what happens.''

Doubt crept into her eyes. ''Jarrett, I don't know....''

''I said we'll see what happens. No pressure.''

Ashley wasn't sure she could trust him. She knew she couldn't trust herself.

But Jarrett was true to his word. At home, they shared a relaxing dinner. Aside from cuddling together on the couch, it could have been like any other night. Ashley was tempted to let it go at that. She knew the call was up to her. The sensible choice would be to take things slow and easy, live with these feelings they had brought out in the open with one another.

For all intents and purposes, she had known Jarrett only a little more than six weeks. To go forward with anything more than an admission of attraction and a few kisses was foolhardy, dangerous to her peace of mind.

She wondered what she would have done in the past.

She wondered what they had done together.

How he had made her feel.

What sound she made when his body moved inside her own.

The suspense was more than she could stand.

So she turned in Jarrett's arms and kissed him with all the fire she was feeling. "Tell me," she murmured as her arms twined around his neck. "Tell me about the first time we made love."

He chuckled. "I'm not sure it was that memorable, Ashe."

"But I want to know." She pressed her lips to the pulse beating at the base of his throat. He smelled of their afternoon. Like the leather jacket he had worn, the popcorn they had shared, the excitement of the ball game. His scent, combined with the feel of his heart beating hard beneath her hand, made her bold. "Show me how it was," she said, rising up to look him in the eye. "Show me how we made love."

"Ashe." Her name was half sigh, half groan. "Are you sure?"

"I want to know. If I can't remember, I want you to show me." She drew away and got to her feet, holding out her hand to him. "Come on."

They went to her room. Jarrett said he had fantasized about knocking down her closed door for too long to go upstairs to his bed.

He threw back the yellow comforter and, kissing her, laid her back against the floral sheets. Only one bedside lamp was on, so the light was soft, romantic. His touch was equally tender.

"Is this the way it was?" she asked. "Remember, you're supposed to be telling me a story."

"It's hard to think about what happened then. Wouldn't you rather concentrate on the here and now?"

She waggled a finger at him. "You said you'd tell me."

He sighed, then bent to kiss her. "I can assure you I wasn't this smooth."

"I'm sure I didn't care."

"We were both kind of upset."

Ashley pulled away from him. "Why?"

"It was the spring after we met. We had planned our wedding for August. Gray was giving us fits, trying to get us to call it off. We decided to forego the hassles and just go get married."

"But we didn't."

"We spent the night together first. Then we saw Kathryn, to get your dress. She talked us out of the elopement."

"And that was the first night we were lovers?" Swiftly, she counted months from the autumn dance where they met until the following spring. "We had waited until then?"

Again Jarrett's devilish grin appeared. "Not by any choice of mine."

"So you put the pressure on."

"I had decided I was willing to wait." He brushed

her hair away from her forehead. "Then you said the magic words."

Ashley slipped her arms around his shoulders. "Where were we?"

"A truly second-rate motel."

"Did we care?"

"You were all I cared about."

The raw emotion in his voice brought a lump to Ashley's throat. If he had felt that way about her, how had they drifted apart?

Jarrett stretched out beside her, head braced on one arm, the other hand trailing down her side. The air was thick with the memories he was trying to share with her. "I wanted it to be special," he whispered.

"So it was my first time."

He nodded.

"But not yours."

He grinned. "Might as well have been. I was pretty damn nervous. We had come so close to making love so many times. I couldn't believe it was really going to happen. I kept waiting for you to call a halt to the whole thing."

"Don't tell me I was a tease."

"You simply kept your head when I lost mine."

"But not that night."

In answer, he leaned forward and claimed her mouth once more. His hand rested on her stomach. The kiss deepened, and his fingers spread upward till he was cupping her breast. His thumb stroked across her nipple, and she winced.

He drew back quickly. "What's wrong?"

"I'm a little sensitive. The baby, you know."

Jarrett looked uncertain, eyeing her as if she were uncharted territory he wasn't sure how to reach.

"Don't worry," she assured him. "I won't break."

"I don't want to hurt you."

"Is that what you said to me that first night together?"

"Of course."

"And I bet you didn't."

Slowly, with great care, he cupped her breast once again. His eyes were very dark in the shadowy light, but they gleamed as he touched her. This time, her nipple simply hardened, blooming under his gentle ministrations. Luxuriating in the pleasure of his touch, she didn't protest when he drew her sweater up and over her head.

Only when her bra was unclasped did shyness take over. She covered her breasts with her hands. "Could you get the light? Please."

He laughed. "That's exactly what you said that night."

"I wasn't a pregnant cow then."

"You aren't now." As if to prove his words, Jarrett bent forward to kiss the small but pronounced swell of her belly. He pushed her denim leggings downward, and his tongue trailed in their wake. A flush started low and radiated up the body that was laid bare to his gaze.

"You're beautiful," he murmured as he finished

undressing her. His hands pushed hers away from her breasts. "Completely beautiful."

She gasped as his mouth opened on one nipple. He didn't hurt her this time. The stimulation was simply so intense, she could barely breathe, especially when one of his hands drifted downward in a slow, smooth spiral across her stomach. Inside her, the baby moved.

Jarrett lifted his head and jerked his hand away. "I felt that."

Laughing, she drew his fingers back to her. "You couldn't have."

"But I did."

"Maybe." Without thought, she guided his hand downward, toward the heat that radiated from between her thighs.

He sighed with pleasure. "You weren't so bold all those years ago, Ms. Grant."

"It just feels like the thing to do."

"Hold on one minute." Jarrett sat up, doffing his sweatshirt in one smooth motion. The rest of his clothes were dispatched just as fast.

Ashley caught one brief glance of his muscled torso and jutting sex before he lay down and took her into his arms. "Are you ready for the rest of the show-and-tell?"

Glorying in the feel of hard male flesh pressed against her own heated skin, Ashley nodded. "You could go strictly with the show, if you're tired of talking."

In answer, his mouth settled on hers. This kiss was

like a drug, sending her on a dizzy descent into a world where the senses of taste and touch, scent and sound, were heightened beyond her wildest dreams.

Jarrett kissed her everywhere. With his clever tongue, he stripped away her last, lingering inhibitions. From her lips to her breasts, to the moist cleft at the juncture of her thighs, she offered herself up to the exploration of his mouth and his touch.

She reached for him time and again. He brushed her hands away and said this time was for her, the way it had been that first time.

With his touch, he brought her to climax. Her slide into pleasure was breathless and complete. Ashley couldn't stop the moan that tore from her throat or the way she bucked and rolled against Jarrett's hand, shamelessly milking every scrap of rapture from the moment. She was still trembling when he lifted her body and surged upward and into her.

The first thrust stole her breath again.

Jarrett pulled himself up, so that they faced one another, torso to torso, her legs straddling his hips. Her hands tightened on his sweat-glazed shoulders. Their gazes locked.

"It wasn't this good the first time," he muttered.

"I don't think I care."

He began to move. Stretching her. Filling her. Taking her even higher than before. He climaxed with one long, wrenching groan, a rush of euphoric release.

They tumbled from the heights together. Slowly,

she slipped to his side, her breathing ragged, her emotions swirling.

When she might have spoken, he pressed his fingers gently against her lips. "Don't, Ashe. Don't talk it to death. Let it be for a few minutes."

He pulled the covers around them. Ashley lay in his arms while the world settled. The rhythm of her heart steadied. Her brain, fogged by desire and anticipation, cleared. In mere moments, she went from contentment to panic. Dear God, what had they done?

As always, Jarrett was able to read her mood. "Don't do it," he said when she shifted slightly away from him. "No regrets, please."

She started to say it was fear, more than regret, coursing through her, but she didn't get a chance. The ring of the telephone cut her off.

"Damn," Jarrett muttered, reaching for the bedside receiver. He listened for a moment, then sat up, instantly alert. His questions were terse and professional and ended with "I'll be right there."

Ashley pushed herself up, tucking the covers under her arms.

"I have to go," he said, unnecessarily. "Emergency." He paused to kiss her, then got up out of bed and grabbed his clothes. "Greta's taking you to work in the morning, right?"

"You think you'll be gone all night?"

"Maybe." In the doorway, he hesitated, his gaze on her. "I'm sorry about this."

She waved him off. "Go on. Someone needs you."

His smile was bright enough to light up her heart, but not still her anxiety. "I'll talk to you tomorrow. Get some sleep now."

She slipped back under the covers, listening as he pounded up the stairs. She heard water running, more footsteps, then he was downstairs, calling out a last goodbye before the front door closed behind him.

One arm curved around her belly as she turned on her side and drew her legs upward. Tonight, of all nights, why did someone need Jarrett more than she did? She wanted him here, so they could talk this thing through. Decide what had possessed them to jump into this intimate situation. Figure out where the hell they should go from here.

Ashley expected to lie awake for hours. But she soon slept as peacefully as the child who rested in her womb. Her subconscious, however, appeared to have been working all night. She awakened in the predawn hours with one thought echoing through her head.

She and Jarrett had made a mistake. A terrible mistake.

The night Jarrett spent in surgery was what he had been trained for, what he professed to love doing. With infinite patience and painstaking care, he put together the torn features of the young woman who lay on the operating table.

He knew surgeons who didn't think of their patients as people. To them, broken and diseased bodies were no more than mechanical parts that required repair. But early on in his training, Jarrett had realized he couldn't be so detached. He couldn't separate the ripped and bleeding face of this woman he labored over, this Toni Alonzes, from the person she might be. She was someone's daughter. Perhaps someone's wife. Their sister. Their mother.

She could be Ashley.

This last thought crept in after the surgery was over. He was checking on Toni one last time when a nurse gave him the details of what had happened to her. The police had discovered her in an alleyway along one of Dallas's meaner streets. Someone had taken a razor to her face, slicing her cheek, forehead and neck.

"Poor kid." The nurse shook her head as she adjusted one of the IVs. "ER's supervising nurse said that by the date on her driver's license, she's just nineteen, and judging from the photograph, beautiful."

"Maybe she'll be beautiful again," Jarrett murmured as he signed off on her chart.

The nurse shook her head. "You may have put her face back together, Dr. Mac, but her wounds are deeper than that."

Jarrett lingered, studying the still form under the crisp white sheets.

Ashley had been found on a street, too. Her body intact, but her mind ripped apart.

What had led each of them to such a terrible juncture?

He shook his head and turned away from his patient. He was crazy to be obsessing over such matters this morning, especially after last night with Ashley. What had happened to her while she was missing wasn't nearly as important as what happened today and tomorrow and the next day. Last night had sent them down a new path.

He hadn't expected to make love to her. When he had told her in the Jeep that there was no pressure about anything, he meant it with all his heart. Sex wasn't the object here. A bonus, maybe, but not the goal.

They were going to get this right this time. He wasn't a randy kid any longer. He wasn't a self-involved, self-righteous intern who had just discovered he held some power over life and death. He was a man who had lived without Ashley in his life, who had faced the possibility that he might have sent her to her death. He knew that emptiness. He liked having her back where she belonged. He didn't care about her past. He couldn't concern himself about the father of her child.

She was his Ashley. As perfect as she had always been.

He had just enough time to grab a quick nap in the doctors' lounge before his morning routine. What he really wanted was to go home and crawl back in bed with Ashley. But that would have to wait.

He woke, got a shower and changed into the fresh

clothes he had brought along before leaving to see patients. It was midmorning when he got to the office. Ashley was at her post, consulting with a nurse over a patient's file. He wished like the devil that she were alone, that he could kiss her senseless and whisper a reminder of last night.

He had to settle for a brief and unsatisfying "Good morning."

Ashley didn't quite meet his eyes. Her face pinkened as she handed him a sheaf of messages. "How's the emergency patient doing?"

"Stable. We'll have to see if I worked any magic on her." His gaze lingered on Ashley. He couldn't stand this impersonal chitchat. "Can I see you for a minute?"

She sent a glance toward the nurse, whose expression was one of bland disinterest. After a moment's hesitation, Ashley followed him to his office.

"You okay?" he asked as he shut the door.

"Why shouldn't I be?"

Something in her tone made him pause. "No reason." He set his briefcase on the desk.

"Is there something you wanted?" Her voice was much too polite.

"Yeah," he murmured. "I'd like for you to look at me."

With obvious reluctance, she raised golden-hued eyes to meet his gaze.

"You're angry about something."

"I don't want to talk about this here."

"But I want to know why you're upset."

"We don't need to discuss our personal life at the office."

"The door is closed."

"And everyone is probably wondering why."

"To hell with everyone. Tell me what's wrong."

Her hands clenched at her sides. "I'm concerned about what happened last night. I think it was a mistake."

"In what way?"

"It was too fast."

He couldn't stop his grin. "We'll take it slow next time."

She made a sound of protest. "Don't joke about this."

She was really, really upset. He took her hand as he settled on the edge of the desk. "I'm sorry. I'm not joking. I'm taking what happened between us very seriously. It was a big deal, not a joke and certainly no mistake."

"With my life in utter confusion, the last thing I need is more turmoil."

"You're no more confused than anyone else on this earth. You're as rational as anyone I know. We went with our feelings last night. We were true to what we wanted. I don't think that's ever a mistake."

Her posture relaxed somewhat, deceiving him into thinking she was soothed. Then she shocked him. "I want to move out. Get a place of my own."

He dropped her hand and straightened from the desk. "That's crazy."

Resentment simmered in her gaze. "A minute ago,

you said I was completely rational. You can't have it both ways."

"There's just no reason for you to move out."

"Putting some distance between us will give us some perspective."

"I don't want perspective. I want you."

"Do you get everything you want?"

The accusatory note in her voice sparked a flash of anger in him. "I hope you're not implying that I seduced you last night."

"Of course not. I was perfectly willing. Too willing. I'm all out of kilter, not thinking about what's best for myself or my baby."

"Your baby is the main reason you need to stay with me. You need my help."

Her eyes narrowed.

Jarrett ignored the warning signs of her temper. "You don't know the city. You don't even have a car yet. You haven't thought this through."

"I'll figure it out."

He threw up his hands. "I promise we won't wind up in bed again until you're sure it's what you want. Just don't go."

She was fuming. "You don't think I can make it without you."

"I didn't say that."

"For all your talk about having faith in me and believing I'm strong, you're just like Gray. You think I'm some fragile creature who will wind up in trouble again if you don't keep a close watch on me."

He tried to calm her down, even as he fought his

own anger. "You're deliberately misunderstanding me."

"I don't think so." She turned on her heel. "I'm going to leave, Jarrett. I'm going to give us the space we need to figure out our feelings for each other."

His temper finally got away from him. "God in heaven, Ashley, don't be so irrational and bullheaded about this."

She paused at the door and slowly turned to face him. Her eyes were very wide. "What did you just say to me?"

Confused, he repeated himself.

Ashley took a step forward. He could see the muscles working in her throat as she swallowed. "You said that to me before."

He frowned. "I did?"

A new emotion took over her features. Wonder, perhaps. "I remember us talking. Arguing, really. You said I was as irrational and bullheaded as Gray always said I was."

Realizing at last what was happening, Jarrett sucked in his breath.

"I was so mad," Ashley continued. "I was leaving. You had made up your mind that we had to postpone the wedding. You had decided we had to wait." She twisted her charm bracelet on her wrist in excitement. "I was so angry I wanted to hit you."

"You remember? You really remember?"

"I practically slammed the door on your hand and drove off."

Jarrett crossed the distance that separated them

with two long strides and caught her up in his arms. "That's how it was. That morning when you left me."

Ashley closed her eyes and held on to him. She had been fooled before, when a small, tantalizingly clear memory had floated to the surface and she expected more to follow. But now she truly believed a floodgate would open and the memories would come rushing in. For the briefest of moments, she could actually feel them pressing down on her.

But the dam in her brain remained tightly closed, as if the memory that had escaped was no more than runoff after a storm.

She looked up at Jarrett, at his expectant, pleased smile, and she wanted to scream. Damn it to hell, she wanted to be whole, to understand who she was. How else was she ever going to trust her emotions? How else would she figure out what they should do?

Pushing him away, she turned to the door again. "I need to think. I'm going back to work."

"But, Ashe—"

"We'll talk about everything else later. Tonight." She closed the door on whatever he tried to say.

Chapter Eight

Ashley spent the rest of the morning avoiding Jarrett. Not too difficult, given his schedule, but she could sense the impatience simmering in him every time their paths crossed. He simply had to understand. Leaping into physical intimacy with him was a huge step. She needed and wanted some time to sort through her feelings.

That unexpected jolt of memory she had experienced had unsettled her further. Her recollection was as free-floating as her ability to call Jarrett by name or the other, small, disjointed sensations of familiarity she had experienced in the past few months. This memory was different. Unlike those vague outlines, she had clear recall of that last morning with Jarrett before leaving for California. She remembered what she had been wearing, what Jarrett had said to her, how angry and hurt she had been.

The prospect of more memories both excited and terrified her. Ashley wondered if she needed some help. Though she knew she hadn't given the psychologist in Amarillo much of a chance, perhaps she could now benefit from some therapy. Dr. Duval had recommended a Dallas psychologist. Perhaps it was time to consider making an appointment.

When she returned from lunch, Jarrett was waiting at her cubbyhole, his expression uncertain. "Isn't this afternoon your obstetrician's appointment?"

Ashley had forgotten. She groaned, dreading the prospect of adding a gynecological exam to this stressful day. "I'd really like to put it off."

"Getting you this appointment wasn't easy, and we cleared my schedule, as well." Though the OB–GYN was an old friend of Jarrett's, she was sought after. He had called her personally and filled her in on Ashley's situation.

Though acknowledging the trouble he had gone to, Ashley still wanted out of this. Jarrett's unflinching regard told her she didn't have much of a choice unless she wanted to make a scene. So she agreed, but she wanted to go alone.

"I'm going with you," Jarrett insisted.

Ashley glared at him; he scowled back.

He said, "Dr. Winslow's office is in the medical center at the hospital complex. I'll go straight from your appointment to check on last night's emergency patient. Then we'll go home.'' A suggestion of threat colored these last words.

Anger made Ashley flush. She hated having him dictate to her what she should do, but arguing was probably as fruitless as it was childish, especially here at the office. His attitude was making her feel as hemmed in as she had at Gray's.

Thankfully, they exchanged no more than a dozen words on the drive to her appointment. Ashley liked petite, blond Dr. Winslow immediately. She accepted Ashley's amnesia without blinking an eye, and her manner in the exam room was patient and respectful.

Once the physical exam was over, Jarrett asked to join them in Dr. Winslow's office to ask questions and discuss any concerns. Jarrett took over the conversation, and Dr. Winslow's gentle blue eyes turned steely. ''Jarrett, Ashley is the one having this baby. She might want to get a word in edgewise.''

Mouth thinning, he shut up.

''Thank you.'' Ashley turned a cold shoulder his way and smiled at the doctor. ''Although I think he has covered everything from diet to exercise to your recommendations for Lamaze classes, I appreciate being asked to participate.''

The corners of Dr. Winslow's mouth quirked as she looked from Ashley to Jarrett and back again. Clearly, she had not missed the undercurrents at work in this room. Moreover, she had just examined Ashley on a most intimate level, and she had answered Ashley's questions about sexual activity during pregnancy. Though Jarrett had presented Ashley as an old friend, with him acting like a snarling, possessive guard dog, Dr. Winslow had to be wondering about their relationship.

The doctor pushed away from her desk with quick, efficient movements. "Ashley, you're doing great. Work on holding the weight down. Make an appointment for next month before you leave. You'll be at almost six months then, and we'll do another sonogram, maybe even figure out if you're carrying a boy or a girl. Feel free to call me with any concerns, anytime."

Within minutes, Ashley and Jarrett were outside, moving through a glass-covered walkway that connected the office building to the hospital.

Halfway there, Jarrett took hold of Ashley's arm and drew her to the side. "I didn't intend to take over back there."

Stubbornly avoiding his gaze, Ashley fingered the strap of her handbag and stared down at the traffic passing on the street below them.

"Is there nothing I can do or say to you today that's right?"

The weariness in his voice made her look at him. "I don't want to fight with you."

"Nor I you."

"Then don't be so bossy. At least listen to me before you start telling me what to do."

He started to say something, then reconsidered. "Come on. I need to see my patient, and we'll go home. We'll talk."

Slightly mollified, Ashley went with him up to the

intensive-care floor. He told her she could wait outside, but curiosity prompted her to accompany him into a large circular room rimmed with glass-walled patients' cubicles. No one questioned her because she was with Jarrett.

As he flipped through his patient's chart, he introduced her to Candy, a plump black nurse who manned the central monitoring station. Then he disappeared into one of the cubicles. All Ashley could see of the patient was a bandage-wrapped head. She turned back to the nurse.

Candy gave her a friendly smile. "Dr. Mac's one of our favorites around here."

"He's a good doctor."

"The best." Candy's smile dimmed, however, as she nodded toward the room Jarrett had entered. "I hope he can do something for this poor girl."

Ashley hesitated to ask for details, but Candy was less discreet. Toni Alonzes's sad story made Ashley shiver. She couldn't put the girl out of her mind, especially after Jarrett emerged from the cubicle with his features set in grim lines.

The fate of this young woman made Ashley quiet and contemplative on the drive home. Little more than a month ago, Ashley's own situation had seemed nearly as impossible. Yet it could have been worse. Despite her pregnancy, there had been no signs that she had been forced into the horrors of selling herself. No disease. No sign of rape or recent sexual contact. Just a lump on her head and blank space where the details of her life and identity should be. Ashley couldn't help feeling a kinship with Jarrett's patient.

After she and Jarrett arrived home, he went straight upstairs. Ashley wondered if the two of them might simply retreat to their respective corners for this evening. She would welcome the respite. But he reappeared, freshly showered and in jeans and an old T-shirt, while she was preparing a simple dinner.

"I'll do this." Jarrett took a platter of marinated chicken out to the grill on the deck. He cooked while she set the table and added Caesar dressing to the salad.

They ate in the same near silence in which they had come home.

Only when he began gathering china and silverware did she speak. "You have to be exhausted. I'll clean up."

"It's no problem."

She gently but firmly pulled her plate out of his hands and got to her feet. "I insist."

"No matter what I do today, it's wrong, isn't it?"

Sighing, Ashley set the dishes on the counter between the dining room and the kitchen. "Let's leave this discussion for another time, please. We're both too tired to do it justice."

"So we just let this fester another day?"

"'Festering' isn't the term I would choose. Maybe we should both just cool off."

"If we cool off, do you think we'll forget what happened last night?"

She didn't answer, concentrating on removing the serving dishes from the table instead.

Jarrett wouldn't let it rest. "Do you think if you move out, I'll want you any less? Will you stop wanting me?"

"Want isn't the issue." Her chest tightening, Ashley almost gave in to her irritation. Couldn't Jarrett see how deepening their relationship complicated matters? She had enough on her plate without complicating the mix. She had sworn not to become emotionally involved with him, to keep their interaction on a friendly level. Then she had lost her head and slept with him anyway.

She attempted a calm explanation. "I moved here so that I could have the time and space to recapture what I've lost, the freedom to discover who I am. I admit I wanted to be with you. You made me feel safe, while encouraging me to figure out what I was going to do with the rest of my life. With or without my memories, you've always made me feel I had a future."

"That's all I intended to do, Ashe. I just wanted to help you."

"But I always knew there was a danger. I knew we had a history, even one I couldn't remember. And I was attracted to you, too, right from the moment you found me in Canada."

"The connection we felt from the start shows your mind didn't blank out everything."

"But from the first night here, I've been thinking

in terms of us—you and me—instead of in terms of me alone. I've gotten things all out of order.''

''This is my fault.''

''No, it's not,'' she protested. ''Please, let's not go through this again. I *chose* to sleep with you.''

''Because that's what I wanted.''

A dull throb started in her temples, but again she managed to keep her voice level and free of anger. ''Why is it that you always think you're in control?''

His eyebrows drew together. ''I don't.''

''Then why can't last night be about what I chose, instead of what you pushed for?''

She held up her hand, stopping him before he could form another denial. ''You seem to think you're in the driver's seat in every situation. Whether it's what happened last night, or what happened when I left for California and disappeared. You blame yourself for that, as if I had no choice about where I went and what I did.''

''I pushed you into that choice,'' Jarrett insisted. ''If I had given you what you wanted, you wouldn't have gone.''

''But you didn't want what I did. So you were right not to marry me.''

Jarrett pushed away from the table and stood. ''I should have handled it better. I should have held on to you.''

Irritation pushed past her control. ''I hate it when you say that you should have *handled* me. Like I was something you needed to train or pacify.''

''That's not what I mean.''

"But it's how you sound," she retorted.

His voice rose, as well. "I'm sorry, all right? I'll try to watch the semantics."

It was the attitude underlying his choice of words that bothered Ashley. But again, she chose not to fight. "Okay. Fine. Let's leave that alone. The point is that I did leave you. We can't change what happened."

He didn't seem to be listening to her. "I was a fool that morning. I was sure you would come back. But you called my bluff. You left. You were gone." His voice broke on that last word, and she looked up in surprise. His eyes were bright, his hands gripping the upholstered back of the dining-room chair. He looked so sad, so tortured. Her heart turned over, but she didn't know what to say.

Jarrett cleared his throat, getting hold of his emotions. "That patient I saw at the hospital today made me think of you."

Amazed as always at the way their minds worked in sync, Ashley nodded. "I can see why." She explained that the nurse had relayed part of the young woman's story to her.

"That girl could have died in that alley. Bled to death. As it is, her face..." He sighed. "I did what I could. I'll do more. But whoever cut her wanted to inflict some lasting damage."

"The nurse said she's just nineteen."

"And all alone. I can't help wondering why."

There were untold numbers of reasons. Just as there were reasons why Ashley had not reached out to her own family or to Jarrett during the years she was gone.

Lines deepened around Jarrett's mouth. "The people who let this happen to her should pay for their mistake."

Ashley knew he was saying he should pay for what had happened to her. "Please, don't blame—"

He cut her off. "No matter what you say, I will always blame myself. That's about the only thing your brother and I have in common—the guilt we both feel."

"Both of you need to get over yourselves," she snapped.

Jarrett almost smiled. The comment was so typical of Ashley, and showed she was returning to her normal self a little more each day. Her memories were returning, as well, and the pieces of her life would soon fit back together. Some of those pieces could be difficult to accept. His responsibility was to help make that process as painless as possible.

He thought she needed to know where he stood on their relationship, what he wanted. He took her hand.

As if she could anticipate what he was about to say, her eyes deepened from gold to amber. "Jarrett, please—"

"Just listen for a minute," he said around the lump that was in his throat. "Last night was a mistake."

Ashley's shoulders relaxed a bit. "I'm so glad you see it that way."

"It's not that I regret making love to you." He caught her other hand in his, squeezing her fingers. "I could never regret sharing anything that beautiful with you. But I didn't go about things in the way that I should have."

Her chin angled upward. "Would you have stopped it from happening? There were two of us involved in last night's decision."

"But you're right to say things have gotten all out of order between us. I started everything yesterday afternoon. I put the rush on you."

That she didn't deny. She waited, her expression both expectant and fearful.

He cleared his throat. "Last night wasn't about just one night. It was about wanting each other, yes, but I hope it was a whole lot more. I should have made that clear before we made love." He hesitated, trying to read the look in her eyes. "I want to make a commitment to you. I want to offer you what I didn't three years ago. What I should have offered."

She pulled her hands from his.

But he was determined to tell her what he had decided earlier today. "I want to marry you."

Her sharp intake of breath was the only sound in the room.

Jarrett forced out a laugh. "That's not exactly the way you reacted the first time I asked for your hand."

Beneath her simple blue sweater, Ashley's breasts rose and fell with her rapid breathing. She looked everywhere but at him.

He reached out and touched her cheek, practically forcing her to look at him. "Don't tell me you're not tempted."

Her smile was tremulous. "Of course I'm tempted."

"Then say yes."

"I can't."

He went straight for her weakest spot. "Think of your baby." Jarrett let his hand drift down to her gently swelling stomach. "This little guy needs a father."

"He—or she—may have a father waiting somewhere."

"The likelihood of that grows a little dimmer each day, don't you think?"

"But if he's somewhere, waiting—"

Jarrett cut to the chase. "The point is that I'm right here. I want this to be *my* child. I want to watch your belly grow, be with you when he's born. I want to wake up in the middle of the night when he cries, rock him to sleep. I want to play catch and put together ridiculous Christmas toys and put him through school and watch him get married and become a father himself. I want to be his father."

The picture he painted was tempting. More than tempting. It was out-and-out emotional blackmail. Ashley realized Jarrett knew all the right buttons to push, all the points to press to make her bend to his will. Not that his will was altogether unpleasant. But did he always have to take control? Set the timetable?

Before she could reply to him, he continued his plea. "Say yes to me, Ashley. Say yes, and you will never wind up alone again. Some other man may be your baby's biological father, but he let you go, and he hasn't come looking for you. He doesn't deserve you, damn it.

"Be my wife, and you and your child will never want for anything. Ever. Not as long as I'm alive or even when I'm not—"

"Stop it." Voice rising, Ashley pressed her hands to her face. "Please just stop for a minute. My head is spinning. I can't think."

"Don't think. Just say yes."

"No." With several deep breaths, she visibly took hold of herself. "I won't just say yes, not like I just jumped into bed with you last night. We're going to think about this. Talk about this."

"You're not saying no."

She looked into his eyes for a long, long moment. God, but she was weak where he was concerned. "I'm not saying no."

Over her protests, he pulled her into his arms and kissed her. She resisted at first, then kissed him back. But only for a minute.

She pulled away. "Please give me time, Jarrett. Let me sort through some things. My memory's starting to return. Let's go with that for a while."

"Don't be cautious. Don't be sensible. That was my mistake the first time around. I let logic override what we felt for each other."

The memory that had returned to her this morning—of their argument before she left him—trickled back to Ashley again. If she remembered correctly, caution had been his primary concern the morning of what should have been their wedding day. Now he was the reckless one, pushing her for answers she didn't have, a commitment she wasn't sure she was ready to make.

"We can't be crazy," she said. "We can't pretend there isn't a lot to consider."

"Why?" he demanded, eager to cut through the details. "Why not pretend we're back where we were a long time ago? Why not just pretend you never went away?" He stepped close to her once more, one hand settling on her stomach, the other in her shining, honey hair. His voice dropped to a whisper. "Pretend, Ashe. Pretend this baby is mine. Pretend everything is perfect, like it was once before."

She swayed, both mentally and physically.

But something held her back.

"I can't," she murmured. Misery swam in her eyes. "The first day I came home, when I pretended to recognize that painting in my old room, you told me lies wouldn't make this situation easier. You were right. I can't pretend. I did leave, and this isn't your child, and there's more to think about than how wonderful it feels for you to hold me."

Jarrett searched her features but sensed he had pushed as hard as he could for now. Sighing, he pulled her close and pressed a kiss to her forehead. "I wish I could put everything together for you."

She tipped her head back. "You want to repair me like you repaired your patient's face last night."

He didn't want her to see it that way. "Don't think of yourself as flawed."

"What else would you call me? I don't have a memory. I don't know where I was or what I did for nearly three years."

Jarrett didn't bother telling her it wouldn't matter to him what she had done. But he had realized sometime during this long, frustrating day that he had to *show* her how much he cared. He had to prove himself to her. If that meant backing off and giving her space, he would do it.

There was one last point he wanted to get straight. "Whatever else you decide, you're forgetting about moving out of here."

Ashley's expression grew stormy once again. "You don't decide where I live."

"But I can beg you to stay, can't I?" He took a step back. "If it will make you feel better, I promise you hands off. No pressure whatsoever."

"No pushing me for an answer I just can't give you yet?"

"No pressure," he repeated.

She lifted one skeptical eyebrow. "That's what you said yesterday."

"This time I mean it. I want you to stay here. I need you to stay here. I'd go crazy with worry if you left. Honestly, Ashe—"

"All right already." She threw up her hands. "I'll stay for now."

"And I'll stay in my own bed."

Ashley looked doubtful. Maybe even somewhat regretful. Jarrett used all his self-control not to pounce on her hesitation.

He kept a tight leash on himself all that night.

And the next day.

For what felt like an endless week.

He started hating her bedroom door again. He willed it off its hinges. He imagined storming it open.

Then he imagined her in that bed with him. Naked. Warm. Vibrant and loving. The Ashley he had let go. The woman to whom he wanted to make up for the biggest mistake he had ever made.

He could never let her go again. He had so much to make up for.

Ashley knew Jarrett was having difficulty holding back, not pushing for an answer and not pressing for intimacy. She knew because she felt the same way herself.

He simply had no right to be so attractive. At home, especially in the mornings, he could be a rumpled, grumpy little boy, a pose she found particularly appealing. Yet overlying that was a blatant masculinity that wasn't boyish in the least. It was impossible to forget, for even a moment, that he was all male. Supremely confident. More than a little bit dangerous to her peace of mind.

At work, he was a polished and poised professional, a man she admired as much for the skill in his hands as for his way with his patients. He was in control, decisive and firm. But he took the time to be kind. For the little burn victim he had told Ashley about on her first day of work, he shopped to find the exact Barbie doll she confessed she had been pining for since the fire that had destroyed her family's home. He was gentle with the aging beauties who came to him seeking a magic eraser for the lines left by time. He shared the grief of those who had to confront the limitations of what medical science could do.

The irony of his complex appeal was not lost on Ashley. The tender side of his nature melted her heart, even as she resented the brash confidence and take-charge manner that led him to try and make all the decisions for their lives.

No matter what mode he was in, he was difficult for Ashley to resist.

And she had to wonder, why did he want her?

The question nagged at her all during the week after he asked her to marry him.

Her biggest worry was that Jarrett wanted to marry her simply because of his guilt. He would deny that if she asked. She didn't think he could even admit such a thing to himself. But it was a strong possibility and one she had to give plenty of thought to. Guilt was the wrong reason to be married, the wrong atmosphere in which to bring up a child.

Sex, of course, was a compelling reason. Clearly, their physical connection was strong. All Jarrett had to do was look at her with his long-lashed brown eyes, and she was hot. She knew how she reacted when he touched her. She knew he reacted the same way to her. Was it simple chemistry? Was it more complex? A mixture of history and the forced intimacy of living and working together?

But sex was no more an acceptable foundation for marriage than guilt. What could Ashley, a woman pregnant with another man's child, a college dropout lacking in memories, offer a talented, brilliant young surgeon?

The question pushed Ashley into some deep self-assessment.

Without being vain, she could admit she was an attractive woman, especially since she had started wearing clothes she chose for herself instead of others' castoffs. Greta, who was an offbeat sort of person herself, termed Ashley's style "funky." She did find herself drawn to unexpected pairings of textures and colors.

Growing bold during the next few days, she followed her instincts in picking out some colorful touches for Jarrett's bland home. A jade vase she and Greta filled with wheat. A garland of silk ivy she tossed over the white swags at the windows. A stack of multicolored hat boxes in one corner. A crafty hiding place for the hideous chrome-and-glass candlesticks on the mantel.

Making those small decisions gave her a big thrill. It felt so wonderful to say, *I like this. I don't like that. This suits me.* Jarrett seemed as pleased with her happiness as with the changes. He gave her carte blanche and a budget with which to do anything she wanted to the condo.

So often he said that she was acting like her old self. That she hadn't really changed. She knew that couldn't be true. Even if she didn't know herself, the experience she had been through had to have changed her. Indeed, as she went over all she knew about the young woman who had run away from Jarrett, Ashley decided she hoped she had changed. Become stronger. Not quite so reckless.

A person was emerging from the ashes of the identity. Family and friends had told her she used to be headstrong, impulsive and flighty. She knew she was still stubborn. Refusing to give in to Jarrett's proposal showed that much. Agreeing to move to Dallas and then sleeping with Jarrett so quickly proved she might still be spontaneous. But she wasn't so sure the capriciousness remained.

For one thing, she was utterly dedicated at work. She concentrated fiercely and took pleasure from being thorough and accurate. She liked the fast-paced atmosphere. Most of all, she relished her contact with patients. She found satisfaction in arranging tests and procedures that fit in with their lives, as well as Jarrett's schedule. She was genuinely interested in their stories, their troubles.

Greta and some of the other office employees complimented her often, said she had a knack for dealing with difficult people. Ashley's pleasure at their praise was all out of proportion, she knew. But she loved being good at what she was doing.

Friday evening, she went with Greta for dinner and a movie. Jarrett looked unhappy, especially when she didn't get in until nearly midnight. He fussed about the baby and how tired she must be. Ashley laughed, gave him a kiss and went to bed.

She woke up on Saturday morning and felt almost…normal. Whatever normal was. Most of all, she felt strong and determined.

She wanted to do one thing today. Go to the hospital and see Toni Alonzes.

Ashley had been ignoring this compulsion all week. She had been unable to get Toni out of her mind all week long. She kept thinking she and this young woman might have something to say to one another. She knew Jarrett would disapprove, would tell her not to get upset over someone she didn't know. That's why she wasn't going to discuss this with him. She didn't need his permission, his blessing.

He left to play racquetball after his rounds on Saturday morning. Ashley dressed carefully in a new plum-colored dress with a long floral vest, then called a cab. She knew Toni had been moved from ICU to a room yesterday. During the drive to the hospital, she rehearsed what she was going to say. She almost asked the driver to turn around. For what could she say to this woman, this stranger? There was every reason to expect her to have Ashley thrown out of her room.

The driver let her out at the front entrance. She

went up to Toni's room, rapped on the door and responded to the weak reply by stepping inside.

Toni lay on her side facing the door, her face still wrapped in bandages. Only her mouth and one eye were uncovered. Her hands, which had suffered defensive wounds, were also bound in white.

"Yes," she croaked, one long-lashed dark eye staring out at Ashley. "Who are you?"

Ashley took a deep breath. "You don't know me, Toni, but I work for Dr. McMullen."

"Dr. Mac?" Her voice sounded stronger. "He was here this morning."

"I work for him, and I'm an old friend."

The eye blinked. "So?"

She explained about being with him in ICU and one of the nurses telling her what had happened to Toni, how she had been found near death in an alley.

The young woman lay still beneath the blue hospital sheet. When she spoke, there was an absence of emotion. "So what are you? Some kind of social worker, come to preach at me about the dangers of life on the street?"

"No, I'm not here to lecture you."

"Then what do you want?" Toni turned her head away. "I don't want to see nobody."

"I think maybe you and I have a few things in common."

The eye roamed her way again. Ashley could practically hear the young woman making mental comparisons that didn't add up. "You and me? Like what?"

"Like being left for dead on some street."

A short, considering silence reigned from the bed. Curiosity obviously won out over maintaining the illusion of disinterest. "What happened to you?"

"Can I sit down?" Ashley asked.

Toni gave a grudging consent. Ashley pulled a straight-back chair forward, sat and began to tell her story to this stranger.

Chapter Nine

Early-November dusk was descending over the city before the cab deposited Ashley back at the condominium complex. She paid the fare and walked slowly toward the elevator. Not since her first days in the hospital had she felt this weary.

Jarrett met her at the front door. She could see he was frantic but working hard to hide it. "Where have you been?"

She sent him a distracted glance and handed him the note she had left on the foyer table. "I told you I was going out for the afternoon."

"I didn't expect you to be so late." He hesitated, and Ashley imagined he was trying not to be too overprotective or inquisitive. She had to give him points for attempting to give her the space she had requested.

Tonight, however, she was grateful to walk into this warm, safe home, to be greeted with his concern. So she hugged him.

He seemed surprised. "Is something wrong?"

She shook her head. "I'm just tired."

"You're sure that's all there is to it?"

Going over the emotions that had bombarded her all afternoon was simply more than Ashley could handle right now. "I want to lie down for a while, okay?"

Jarrett's brow remained wrinkled, but he let her go to her room without another protest. She changed to one of the oversize sweat suits handed down from Kathryn. The material was worn to a pleasantly nubby softness and felt good against Ashley's skin. Most of all, it was warm.

During this long afternoon with Toni Alonzes, she had grown cold, chilled by the realities the young woman shared with her. Toni was the product of a broken and abusive home. Until last year, she battled the poverty and indifference of her mother, had stayed in school, worked a part-time job, tried to keep her grades up while caring for her younger siblings. Eventually, she had been overwhelmed by her responsibilities. One bad choice led to another, leading her to the hospital bed where she was today.

Bad choices. As she talked with Toni, Ashley realized how lucky she was that her own bad choices had not brought her to a similar fate.

Once she started talking, Toni had been open and candid about her life on the street. Ashley suspected the young woman hadn't really talked with anyone in a long time. Her family lived in another part of Texas, and she did not want them to know where she was or what had happened to her. They were dead to her now, she said. Ashley did not attempt to tell her what to do. She promised, however, to help Toni in any way she could.

"Why would you do that?" the young woman had asked. "You don't even know me."

"I feel as if I do," Ashley had replied.

Accepting that simple, honest truth, Toni had fallen asleep with Ashley at her side. She didn't seem surprised when she awoke to find Ashley still there.

When Ashley left her with a pledge to come back soon, Toni had even laughed. "I guess you're right. We do have some things in common. Me with my missing face, and you with your missing memories."

Ashley felt those memories would not be missing much longer. Talking with Toni aroused some disjointed and disturbing flashes of being lost and alone, cold and frightened. Ashley couldn't pinpoint the exact place she had been when she experienced those emotions. She didn't know their cause. But her identification with Toni's ordeal was strong.

Shivering, Ashley curled up on her bed. Instinctively, she reached for the telephone and dialed Gray's number.

Kathryn answered, her voice bright and bubbly, raised above a din of laughing youngsters in the background. "Lily's having a sleepover. I'm in the middle of serving pizzas."

"Can Gray talk?" Ashley asked. She didn't want to pull her brother away from his family, but her need to hear his voice was suddenly intense.

Several moments later, he came on the line.

"Are you okay?" Gray asked. "Kathryn thought you sounded upset."

"I'm fine." The minute she offered that reassurance, Ashley's voice thickened against her will. "I'm remembering some things, Gray."

His response was a quick offer to help. "Do you need me there? You want me to come to Dallas?"

She managed a laugh. "What a guy. Always ready to ride to the rescue."

"If you need me—"

"You'd be right here," Ashley finished for him. "I know that, and I appreciate the offer. More than I can say." For some reason, her eyes filled with tears. Not since the night she had first felt her baby move had the need to be close to her family been this strong.

Perhaps Gray sensed her turbulent emotions. He hesitated, then cleared his throat. "We had hoped you might come home this weekend. It's been almost a month."

"It seems longer, somehow."

"Jarrett treating you okay?" The question was transparently casual.

She couldn't resist teasing him. "Aside from ravishing me every chance he gets, yes, he's great."

Gray huffed. "I'm just concerned."

Leaning back against her pillows, Ashley twisted the phone cord and shifted the conversation away from Jarrett. "How did you manage to raise me and Rick all alone?"

"I got through each day. I got up the next morning and started over, just trying to do my best."

"You make it sound too simple." She thought of Toni's parents. "Other people don't succeed."

A pause stretched between them. "Did I succeed, Ashe?"

"You were always there for us, maybe more than we wanted. Why, I remember..." Words trailing away, Ashley sat up, stunned by the turn her mind had taken.

"You remember?" Gray demanded. "What is it? Tell me."

Ashley spoke slowly, trying to put the fragments of memory together. "I was fourteen, I think. I had a teacher...for math, maybe...and I thought he had it in for me."

"Disagreeable little wimp," Gray muttered.

She laughed as all the pieces fell into place. How the flu had kept her out of school for a week, and the teacher gave her only a weekend to make up homework she didn't understand because of the missed classroom time. As a result, she also failed a test. She had tried to reason with the man, but he was dismissive and made a great show of writing a big red F in his grade book right in front of her. That grade meant she would fall from the honor roll and perhaps lose her place in the school's accelerated scholastic program.

The next morning, Gray went with her to see the teacher. After an initial attempt to be polite and talk the situation through was met with cool disdain, Gray leaned across the man's desk, and with deceptive mildness asked if he got his kicks intimidating little girls. Because if he did, Gray was going to spend a lot of time in his face. Gray never raised his voice, would never have raised a hand to the man. But the teacher's demeanor changed in an instant.

At the time, Ashley had been more mortified than grateful, even after the teacher gave her the instruction and time she needed to make up the work.

Now, she saw the action for what it was. The fiercely protective nature of someone who loved her, who would do anything to make sure she got a fair shake.

Dashing tears from her eyes, she said, "I don't think I ever thanked you for confronting that weasel."

"Of course you didn't," Gray retorted matter-of-factly. "You hated me for interfering. You always wanted to handle everything yourself."

"And that's always been the problem between us."

He sighed. "These last few weeks, I've worked real hard at leaving you alone. Some nights Kathryn has to talk me away from the telephone."

"I know it's difficult to go against your natural tendencies. Thanks."

The breath he drew was ragged. "I just want to know you're safe, that's all."

"Try not to worry about me."

"That's like asking me not to breathe."

"Then try not to worry so much."

He chuckled. She could imagine him leaned back in his chair in his study at home, his fine blue eyes crinkled, his strong handsome features relaxing for once.

"Gray, I..." Her words didn't make it around the obstruction in her throat.

"I know," he murmured. "I love you, too, kiddo."

Her laughter was threaded with tears. "It feels good to be sure of something. And I am sure I love you guys."

"We never doubted that for a minute."

"But why did I stay away from you for so long?" The question spilled from a deep well of remorse inside her. She told him about Toni, about the sort of home she had come from and where she had ended up. "I didn't have that to contend with, Gray. So why didn't I come home?"

"Maybe you didn't know where home was."

"I refuse to think I wandered around in a daze for three whole years. That doesn't make sense."

"When you left, you were angry with me for try-ing to tell you what to do with your life. You were angry with Jarrett for the same reason, essentially. That independent streak inside you was operating full blast. It would have taken a lot for you to come running home or to ask for help.''

"So instead, I could have ruined my life.''

"But you didn't. You're going to be just fine.''

The baby stretched in her womb, reminding her of the most important reason to believe him. Ashley smiled. "I hope I can be as good a parent as you are.''

He seemed touched by the compliment. "I wish you didn't have to do this alone.''

Maybe she didn't. As close as Ashley felt to her brother at this moment, she wasn't about to bring up Jarrett's proposal. "I'm not alone. I have all of you guys.''

"You are coming home soon, aren't you? For a visit?''

"Thanksgiving is right around the corner.''

"We'll be ready anytime you want to come.''

Ever since they had found her, Ashley had focused on how her family crowded her, pushed her, needed her to remember, to be the person she had been. She knew she was lucky they had found her, lucky to have them, but until now, she had not truly realized what they had given her.

Determined not to lose her grip on her emotions again, she interjected a note of lightness in her voice. "I love you, big brother. Even when you're driving me insane.''

They ended the call with laughter. Long after clicking off, Ashley sat smiling, feeling the warmth of her family. Eventually, she slipped down against the pillows and fell asleep.

Jarrett knew Ashley was exhausted. He didn't try to wake her for dinner, but peeked in about seven, to find she was lost in deep and peaceful sleep.

He remained strangely on edge, as he had been when Ashley was late coming home. He was unable to concentrate on the medical journals that needed his attention or the thriller he had started reading last month. He ate a sandwich, wandered through the condo, smiling at the new and welcome touches Ashley had added. He thought about going for a run. Anything to shake off this unease.

The last time he remembered feeling quite this undone was in the hotel room in Vancouver, before he found Ashley. Then, as now, he was overwhelmed with the feeling that she needed him.

Another quick check revealed she was still sleeping. He left her alone, not even bothering to shut off the bedside lamp. Telling himself to get a grip, he went up to his bedroom and switched on the television. He fell asleep in the middle of Stallone's latest action effort.

He woke with a start, jarred by a far-off sound. The clock read just after ten. He switched off the television and listened. The house was silent, but anxiety washed over him. Was someone calling his name? Ashley?

The thought sent him downstairs, bare chested and without shoes, clutching a golf putter as a weapon.

He heard nothing until he opened her door. She sat up, screaming.

Tossing the putter aside, he ran to the bed. "It's me, Ashley. It's Jarrett."

She looked at him with dazed eyes until he took her in his arms, stroking her face, touching her. Was she sick? Was the baby okay? All seemed to be fine, except for her bald-faced terror. She trembled as she held on to him. He sat down and pulled her onto his lap.

"It's okay," he whispered, cradling her close. "You're okay, Ashe. I'm here. I'm sorry I scared you."

When her breathing returned to normal, she said, "You didn't frighten me. It was my dream. That stupid nightmare I had all the time in the hospital. I thought it was gone. I haven't dreamed it since I came here."

"What dream is this?"

She colored with embarrassment. "Both Dr. Tiernan and Dr. Duval told me it was a perfectly obvious dream, about when I was lost. It's cold and dark and I'm terrified."

She might have pulled out of his lap, but Jarrett held her tight against his chest. He wanted to make sure she was really okay before he let go. "Is it just the dark you're frightened of?"

"There's a monster there, too," she murmured, looking even more shamefaced. "It's all around me, pushing at the edges of the darkness."

"And what are you doing?"

"Looking for someone. I don't know who. I always wake up before I find out." Sighing, she pushed her hair out of her face. "Dr. Duval thought I was looking for myself."

"Makes sense."

Ashley shuddered. "I thought I was done with that dream. I'm sorry I dragged you in here. Was I screaming?"

"I woke up because I thought someone called my name. When I didn't hear anything, I came down here." Nodding at the discarded putter, he added, "With my trusty weapon, of course."

"You must have been dreaming, as well."

He hesitated as another possibility presented itself to him. A strange and haunting idea. "Maybe I heard you call to me in my dreams."

She drew back in surprise. "You're kidding?"

"Aren't you looking for someone in your dream?"

"Yes, but—"

"Why couldn't it be me?"

Slowly, she said, "I don't remember calling for you. In the dream, I'm just searching, trying to get…" She frowned in concentration. "I think I'm trying to get to some point that's just out of reach."

"Me," he repeated. "You could be calling for me."

"Maybe I really called out and you heard me. You were half-asleep and didn't know where the sound came from."

"I felt this same way that night in Canada before

I found you. I couldn't rest because I couldn't get you out of my mind. I saw a woman at the airport who looked like you. Over and over again, I thought I heard you call for me.''

Ashley continued to regard him with disbelief. ''I would never think of you as someone who would believe in this psychic connection.''

''You see people nearly die and battle their way back, and you start believing in the force of will. The human soul has its own mysterious coping mechanisms.''

She mulled that over. ''So I called out in my dream and you heard?''

''It's not unbelievable.''

''Maybe.'' With gentle hands, she brushed his hair away from his forehead. ''Kathryn told me that you never thought I was dead. You never gave up hope of finding me.''

''I knew you were out there, somewhere. I could feel you.''

''And it was you who found me.''

''By sheer dumb luck. Who knows what would have happened if I hadn't been at that conference? Your picture and story might have eventually reached us, but not for a while.''

''But you were there.'' A line appeared between her eyebrows as she studied him. ''Had you ever been to Canada before?''

''Never. That conference was a last-minute...'' His voice faded as the implication of his words sunk in. The conference had been an impulsive decision, requiring no end of rescheduling and reworking of his schedule. Even on the plane, he had asked himself why it was so important that he attend.

But that was too strange to accept. There was simply no way he had been drawn all the way to Vancouver in order to find Ashley. His being there was a coincidence. Maybe waking up tonight and thinking she called for him was the same.

Shivering, Ashley pressed closer to him. "I'm giving myself the chills just thinking about this."

"It's too strange," Jarrett agreed, though doubts still lingered.

And neither of them made a move to let go of the other.

Expectancy clouded the air.

The tousled bedcovers beckoned.

Jarrett felt his pulse quicken. Heat flowed up his body, radiating from his sex, which grew hard and heavy. He was completely erect from just holding her. What would happen if she leaned forward, if her lips moved a fraction of an inch closer to his own?

He found out, because she did move. She kissed him, and his body pulsed in response.

He jerked back as if burned. "You kissed me."

She threaded her fingers through his hair and drew his mouth back to her own. "Yes, I did." She nibbled at his lips. "I know I shouldn't. But all week, I've wanted to do this." Her tongue traced the outline of his mouth. "And this, too."

Torn between wanting her and obeying the promise he had given her Monday evening, he pulled away again. "Later on, I want you to remember you kissed me. I've kept my word. It's been hands-off all week."

"And you should keep that promise a little more."

Teasing him with light, gentle kisses, she eased off his lap and slowly pushed him back against her pillows. When he reached to pull her with him, she swatted his hands away. "Hands off, remember."

He groaned and clenched his fists at his sides.

"Just relax," Ashley commanded. She leaned over him, her soft hair falling around her face while she kissed him some more.

Relaxing was the last thing on his mind. Especially when her mouth moved from his lips to his chest. His nipples hardened in response. But his near undoing was the hand that drifted low across his belly and dipped downward to cup his full, straining sex.

He reached for her again. Grinning, she pushed his hands back to his sides. "We have an agreement, remember?"

"You're killing me," he growled as she cupped him again.

"This is killing you?" She exerted a slight but altogether delicious pressure on his crotch.

Unable to speak, he closed his eyes.

"We really should ease your pain."

His jeans were already unbuttoned, but she pulled the zipper downward with slow, methodical torture. Then her naughty, questing fingers slid under his boxers and circled his fevered shaft.

Her sigh was as erotic as any kiss.

But not nearly as explosive as the way she next used her mouth.

Jarrett wasn't sure how he got the rest of the way out of his clothes, whether he helped her or she took care of it. He had little idea how hers were disposed of, either. He was sure he violated the no-hands rule. At least a dozen times. To cup her full, ripening breasts. To stroke her pretty, growing belly. To pull her silky, soft body up and under his. To guide his aching, swollen sex into hers.

Once.

Twice.

He probed deeper. Until her legs curved up around his waist and a strangled groan of pleasure tore from her lips. The fingertip hold he had on his own release was broken, and he launched into a free fall of completion.

He was spent, dazed by the sudden intensity of their coupling. Slipping to Ashley's side, he was drowsy with satisfaction. Only she wasn't ready to sleep. She had much more energetic plans to enact.

All Ashley knew was that she wanted to drown in this moment with Jarrett. Fill herself with the taste of his skin, the feel of his touch, the ache he aroused simply with his nearness. When they were this way—naked and alone in the near-darkness—she didn't have to think about what she could offer him. She didn't have to worry he wanted her simply to assuage a misplaced guilt. She didn't have to consider what terrible acts she might have committed in the past. Here, they were simply a man and woman.

And whatever they did, whatever they felt, seemed right and natural and good.

That's why she touched and teased him again. Why she drew him back to the edge of completion. The sensations were so strong she finally pulled away, to roll onto her side and try to catch her breath. Before she could, however, Jarrett positioned himself behind her, pressed her legs apart and filled her again.

The unexpected position, the quick, solid glide of him inside her was enough to scramble what remained of her senses. When their climax had claimed them, she couldn't move. Jarrett wrapped his arms around her, and they slept.

"Are you ever waking up?"

Ashley cracked one heavy-lidded eye toward Jarrett. Chin resting on her bare shoulder, he smiled down at her with charm that was altogether too bright for what must surely be the dark hours of the morning.

"Go back to sleep," she mumbled, pulling the comforter back up to her chin.

"It's almost ten."

Both her eyes flew open, and panic set in until she realized it was Sunday morning. She yawned and stretched and gave Jarrett a considering look as he settled back against the pillows. "Have you been to the hospital this morning?"

"I checked in with all my patients. Everyone was fine, so I crawled back in here with you."

"I'm glad," she whispered, turning to hug him. "You never take it easy."

"You call what went on here last night taking it easy?"

Heat bloomed in her cheeks. But her smile ended in a sigh. "What are we doing, Jarrett?"

"I think it's called being unable to keep our hands off each other."

"I thought I could be strong."

"I thought you could, too."

"Hey, now." She elbowed him in the ribs. "I bet you never intended to be strong at all."

"I'm just a weak male, tempted by a vixen who kisses me." He pressed his lips to hers. "Who strips me naked." He tossed back the covers to their nude bodies. "A woman who has her way with me in about a dozen wanton ways."

"A dozen?"

"We men are prone to exaggeration."

Sweeping a glance down his distinctively male body, she said, "In your case, my dear, exaggeration would be like gilding the lily."

He chuckled and with one quick move, tumbled her onto her back. "I've always heard it's not the size—"

"But what you do with it," she finished, laughing up at him.

"Are you up for another exhibition of my skills?"

"Feels like you're up and ready."

"Standing at attention."

He smothered her giggles beneath another long kiss. Then she began to squirm.

"Slow down," he murmured.

"If you must know, I have to go to the bathroom."

He rolled over and let her escape.

She emerged five minutes later with teeth brushed and her robe on.

"No fair," Jarrett accused, sitting up in bed. "Clothes are prohibited."

Ashley didn't want to confess she was stricken with shyness at having to walk back into the room naked. It seemed that every day her body changed in some new and unexpected way.

"This baby and I must be fed," she told Jarrett. "I eat in clothes."

"We once had a naked picnic."

Her eyes narrowed. "I think that's something you're making up."

"Cross my heart." He grinned so that she couldn't tell if he was lying or not, then swung his feet to the floor. He held out his hand to her. She took it and stepped between his knees.

Tenderly, he opened her robe and pressed his face to her stomach. "Good morning, baby. I hope you're doing okay in there."

The unexpected and sweet gesture tugged at her heart.

Jarrett wrapped his arms around her middle and hugged her close. "I know I promised not to push, but—"

"Yes, you did," she whispered, disentangling

from his embrace. She knew what he was about to say, and she didn't want to deal with it this morning. "Isn't it enough that I've broken my resolve and slept with you again? And it probably won't be the last time, either. You wore me down with your ir-resistible sex appeal, got me to give in and make a move on you."

Her flippant remark was met with stoic concern.

"Jarrett?"

He got up, found his clothes on the floor, pulled on boxers and then jeans. A frown marred his even, handsome features.

She said his name again, took hold of his arm when he might have left the room. "Tell me what's wrong."

He rubbed his jaw, as he did when he was nervous or upset. "I don't want sex to mess things up be-tween us."

She bit her lip. Doubts had plagued her all week about what Jarrett really saw in her, what she offered him besides looks and sex. He seemed to be reading her mind.

"I don't want you to ever think I was wearing you down just for sex," Jarrett said, his brown eyes gleaming.

"I was kidding—"

He cut her off. "We're connected in deeper ways than that. Maybe it's because we got together so young. There's a bond there that can't be broken. I know you don't believe our dreams collided last night. You don't think I was drawn to find you in

Canada.'' He shoved a hand through his hair. ''Hell, I don't know if I believe it, either. But I came running for you. I always will. That's why we should be married.''

She heard what he was saying. She understood he was offering her safety and security, as well as passion.

But she still couldn't accept his proposal.

Not yet.

One word was missing from all his pretty speeches, all his promises.

Love.

He hadn't said he loved her. He wanted her. He had missed her. He felt he owed her. They were connected, bonded. But what about love?

Ashley couldn't ask him for that word. Not when she couldn't offer it in return, either. She had much still to consider about herself. She had to be sure this was true love she felt for Jarrett. Not gratitude. Not merely passion. Not the lingering allegiance of first love.

But was holding out for an elusive, perhaps impossible emotion worth giving up a man like Jarrett? Someone who would love another man's child like his own?

With that question pulling hard at her, she reached out and took his hand. ''I still need time.''

His heart-stopping smile spread across his face. ''I'll wait.''

She rose on her tiptoes to kiss his cheek. ''There's just one other thing I want to make clear.''

He cocked an eyebrow.

"About the sex thing…" She sighed and pretended remorse.

His smile dimmed. "Yeah?"

"Maybe we're better off not resisting it quite so hard."

He grinned his perfect smile. "All that frustration is kind of wearing, isn't it?"

"Exhausting."

Laughing, he swung her up in his arms. "How exhausted do you feel right now?"

"Probably more exhausted than you."

"That sounded like a challenge. Like I need to prove something to you."

She raised her chin. "Bring it on, Dr. Mac. Bring on your best."

Her breakfast ended up very, very late. And Ashley had to agree it was one of Jarrett's very best, shining moments.

Chapter Ten

As Ashley paused in a hallway at the office, Greta reached out and patted her stomach. "Girl, you are blooming."

"A nice way of saying I'm becoming a whale." Ashley cast a rueful glance toward her middle. In the past three weeks, she had gained five pounds. Thanksgiving in Amarillo with Kathryn's sweet-potato casserole and Tillie's pies hadn't helped. Neither did Jarrett's penchant for late-night snacks. Or her own seemingly bottomless appetite.

"You look wonderful. Glowing and happy. Almost like a bride." Greta's last observation was delivered with a not too subtle wink before she continued on her way down the hall and Ashley went to her desk.

Greta was one of the few people who knew exactly how involved Ashley and Jarrett had become. She approved, heartily. Just last week, on what had become a regular evening out with Ashley, Greta had advised her to marry him. She knew all the problems, and she still said they belonged together.

Of course, Greta was a certified romantic and a great believer in psychic connections and the ability of soul mates to find one another. Her opinion was that all the cosmic forces were on Ashley and Jarrett's side.

She had more practical concerns, as well. Having raised a daughter on her own, Greta knew the challenges of single parenthood. She felt Ashley should think of the advantages for her baby a marriage to Jarrett would bring.

He demonstrated his care and concern for Ashley and her child in dozens of large and small ways. Back rubs when she was tired. Plans for a nursery. Talk of a college fund.

Jarrett sincerely wanted this child to be his.

Ashley wished that were true.

But she had begun to believe it was her continuing blankness about the baby's biological father that held her back. Maybe if she could remember something about him, then she could go forward with Jarrett with a clear conscience.

Other memories were coming back. All from the life she led before disappearing. Sometimes a cluster would come to her. Her father's desertion. Rick's birth. Her mother's illness and death. At Thanksgiv-

ing, she remembered other family holidays. Odd bits
and pieces of her life. Good and bad. In the beginning, vague, familiar impressions had seemed un-
important. She realized now that no detail about her
life was too insignificant.

Now she recalled meeting Jarrett, kissing him for
the first time, falling in love with him. Breaking up.
Getting back together with him. How simple it had
seemed. How perfect their future had looked.

She had been so very, very young. Now she knew
nothing was simple.

Close as she felt to her brothers now, Ashley had
not discussed Jarrett's proposal with either of them.
She had asked Jarrett not to say anything to his family, either, and to play it cool during their Thanksgiving visit.

Kathryn had guessed, of course. She offered no
advice other than Ashley following her own heart.

Tillie had penned Ashley in the kitchen at the
Double M, where the extended family had gathered
for dinner. As usual, her sharp, insightful gaze
missed nothing, and she wasn't shy about asking
what was going on with Jarrett. Ashley skipped
around an answer and finally sicced the woman on
Jarrett. Later, he said Tillie's only opinion was that
they ought to marry before the baby was born.

Sound counsel, Jarrett thought.

With her staying with Gray and Kathryn and him
at the ranch for the weekend, Ashley had time to
miss Jarrett. She got a special thrill about coming
home to the condo, which he called *their* home. They

had taken to sleeping in the master bedroom. Little by little, her toiletries and clothes had made their way up, as well. Ashley wasn't sure what she would do when Gray and Kathryn came for a planned visit before Christmas. Jarrett thought she should come clean with them and marry him.

Musing over that thought, Ashley answered the phone that buzzed on her desk. The voice she heard surprised her. It was Toni, calling from the halfway house Ashley and Jarrett had gotten her into for her recovery.

"Can you come by today?" Toni asked.

Ashley frowned. "You sound upset. Everything okay?"

"I just need to talk to you."

"Okay." Ashley promised she would come by during her lunch hour.

She had been planning to visit Toni today or to-morrow anyway. During the past few weeks, she had spent a considerable amount of time with the young woman. Helping Toni deal with the psychological effects of the attack she had suffered made Ashley feel useful. Besides, she truly liked her. Toni had a keen intellect and, when she allowed it to shine through her streetwise veneer, a real sweetness, as well.

When one o'clock approached, Ashley told Greta where she was headed and took a cab through a gray, early-December drizzle. She hoped Jarrett didn't get back to the office before her. He wasn't too keen on her relationship with Toni.

The moment that thought crossed her mind, Ashley became annoyed with herself for worrying about what Jarrett thought about this. So what if he didn't understand the connection she felt to Toni. This was important to her, and he should let it go at that. He was right when he said that, other than being victims of some random violence, she and Toni had little in common on the surface. But Ashley understood the aimlessness and fear that had brought Toni to tragedy. She wasn't sure why she understood those emotions, but she did. She wanted to see that those same feelings didn't suck Toni back into trouble.

Moments later, she stepped out of the cab in front of a Victorian structure near Old City Park. The beautiful old mansion had been saved from the wrecking ball and converted for use as a home for young women seeking a fresh start.

Ashley had done the research to find Tomorrow House. Jarrett had made the calls that landed Toni in one of their few available beds. She could stay only three months, but Ashley hoped that would be enough time for Toni to begin her life anew.

She found the young woman waiting for her in the small side parlor that was used for visitors. Though bandages still covered most of her face, she was no longer so tightly wrapped that speaking was difficult. Ashley couldn't see her whole expression, but she could tell Toni was upset by the way she sat, with her arms folded around her midsection.

"What's wrong?" Ashley asked, taking a seat beside her.

Toni drew in a shaky breath. "My sister has found me."

Ashley knew immediately why this was so distressing. Toni desperately wanted to hide the life she had led from her younger sister, her only full sibling. She felt she had let the girl, Marie, down.

"How did she find you?" Ashley asked.

"She read a newspaper article about the…" Toni swallowed. "About me getting hurt. She started making some phone calls. Marie's a smart girl. She knew how to look."

"Has she been here to see you?"

Toni shook her head. "She's way over at the university in El Paso. She's a freshman. She stayed in school and got herself a scholarship and got out of that house where we grew up."

"Good for her."

"She wants to come and see me," Toni said.

"What do you want?"

"To die." The words were torn from a pain-filled place deep inside Toni.

Ashley laid her hand on the young woman's arm in comfort.

"I don't want Marie to see me like this. To know everything…" Toni drew in a ragged breath. "For so long, I kept wanting to go home to her, you know. I tried to hold down a job and save up enough money to get her out of there. But then, once I started messing up real bad…" Once more, Toni's words trailed away.

"You thought you couldn't face her." An ache

started in the pit of Ashley's stomach. She understood Toni's words on a level deeper than the surface. Because for some reason, Ashley had once felt she couldn't come back to the people who loved her, either. But why? God, how she wanted to know.

With an effort, Ashley turned her attention to Toni's next words. "I didn't know if Marie would want anything to do with me."

"She's called you now. Reached out."

"But once she sees me, hears all I got myself into…"

"She might be more understanding than you think."

Toni paused, her dark gaze lifting to meet Ashley's. "You think I should let her come."

"I'm not going to tell you what to do. But from everything you've said about your family, Marie was the one connection you didn't want to lose."

"It's going to be so hard." Despite her trepidation, it was clear how much Toni wanted to see her sister.

Ashley gave her an encouraging smile. "Whatever you decide, whatever happens, you're strong enough to handle it."

"You think so?"

"Hey, you're tough."

"Yeah." A hopeful sparkle suddenly lit Toni's eyes.

"You two look like you're having a serious conference."

The sound of Jarrett's voice made Ashley swivel

in surprise to the doorway where he stood. "What are you doing here?"

"I called the office just after you left. Greta told me where you were going. I decided to come give you a ride back." Jarrett advanced into the room and smiled at Toni. "I figured I could check on one of my favorite patients, as well."

Toni grimaced. "I don't buy this 'favorite' crap, Dr. Mac."

"I don't make house calls for just anyone," he retorted.

"Gee, I'm so lucky."

"Yes, you are," Ashley asserted. "He's the best."

"Yeah, yeah." The young woman darted a glance between Jarrett and Ashley. "He's here just to pick you up, Ashley. I still got my eyesight. I can see how it is with you two."

"And how is that?" Jarrett asked.

Toni nodded toward Ashley. "She looks like a lovesick puppy."

Ashley colored. "I do not."

"I kind of like that look," Jarrett teased.

With a saucy chuckle, Toni added, "You're no better, Doc. Not with those big cow eyes you make at her."

"Cow eyes?" Jarrett shook his head. "That sounds awful."

Toni rolled her eyes. "It don't look so good, either. You'd better do something soon, like marry this girl."

Ashley protested while Jarrett said, "I'm working on it."

"Speaking of working," Ashley murmured, gathering up her bag. "I'm late."

"All right." Jarrett turned again to Toni. "Can I take a look under those bandages?" He glanced around the room. Though they were alone for now, this was a public area and any of the house's residents or staff could come in. He was sensitive to Toni's fear of others seeing her face. "Want to go somewhere more private?"

Toni hesitated. She glanced at Ashley, who nodded. "We can do it here," the young woman said at last. "I don't guess anyone would have nightmares if they saw me."

"Hardly," Jarrett said.

Jarrett was pleased with the initial healing of her face, but all she could see was a crazy quilt of slashes. They bisected both cheeks, ran across her nose and chin. The most jagged of the cuts dipped low over an eye her assailant had just missed destroying. Other, defensive wounds on her hands and arms were less severe. He directed Toni to a chair beside a window and removed the bandages. Though he was concerned at some puckering in the cut over her eye, Toni's wounds were looking as well as could be expected by this point.

Before he could put the bandages back in place, Toni took a deep breath and turned her face toward Ashley. "Here's the bad news. What do you think?"

If Ashley was horrified, she did an excellent job

of hiding her feelings. She got up and crossed to Toni's side with an encouraging smile. While not downplaying the seriousness of the injuries, she also didn't act as if she was viewing a tragedy.

"You made it out to be worse than it is," she told Toni.

Her chuckle was wry. "Then maybe one day I'll be pleasantly surprised."

"I think that's a definite." Jarrett carefully replaced her bandages and suggested she spend several hours each day with them off. "You don't have to do that in front of others if you're uncomfortable."

Toni nodded, though she gave no real sign that she was going to follow his directive. "Thanks, Doc."

He patted her shoulder. "I'll see you next week."

"And I'll be back Friday." Ashley reached out and took Toni's hand. Jarrett saw that the young woman gripped her fingers.

"Thank you," she whispered. "I'm glad you came. I'll let you know about Marie."

Ashley hugged her, and Toni walked them to the door. She stood there, waving, until they were in his Jeep and on their way.

Sensing Ashley's churning emotions, Jarrett said, "She's doing fine, Ashe."

"It's hard to believe her face will ever be the same."

"Not the same, but whole again."

"There's still a part of her that wishes she had died."

"You're helping her with that. So's the counselor at the house. If Toni wants to, she can turn her life around."

Staring ahead at the rain-streaked windshield, she told Jarrett about Toni's sister. "She's terrified to see her, to share the scars—on her face and on her soul. Fear kept Toni from seeking Marie out a long time ago."

The Jeep was quiet save for the sound of traffic and the steady beat of the wipers.

"I think I was terrified," Ashley said suddenly, filling the silence. "I was afraid to come home, just the same as Toni."

Jarrett spared one sharp look. "You weren't like Toni."

"Did I live on the street? Sell myself? I think the physical evidence showed that was highly unlikely," Ashley agreed. "But I was lost, Jarrett. So lost, my mind decided to shut down."

"Your mind shut down because some thief took your belongings and knocked you on the head."

"You know very well that the blow to my head wasn't severe enough to cause amnesia."

"Head injuries are tricky things."

Ashley gazed at him for a moment, her eyes narrowed. Of all the people in her life, Jarrett had acted the least frightened of the reasons why she had lost her memory, of the events of her missing years. Indeed, he kept insisting she would remember, that it all would come back. But perhaps he was more fearful than anyone else. More fearful than he could admit even to himself.

Maybe he would be just as happy to never know the truth.

She said nothing, didn't press the issue. But the very idea disturbed her in some fundamental way. As long as that part of her past remained buried, Jarrett could mold their future accordingly. Without the baby's biological father to intrude. Without unpleasant realities. The two of them could go back in time, in a sense.

If she never remembered, Jarrett could eventually stop feeling he was responsible for something terrible.

He could marry her. Take care of her and the baby and take care of his own misplaced guilt.

That realization made Ashley's head pound. It ate away at her for days.

Jarrett knew Ashley was fretting over something, though she wouldn't talk about it. He chalked her moodiness up to her advancing pregnancy and tried to concentrate on pleasant matters. Like her sonogram scheduled for later in the week. He bet her a week's worth of kitchen chores that the baby was a boy.

And he won the bet.

Sitting beside Ashley, staring at the screen where her child was revealed in all his masculine glory, Jarrett didn't think he could have been any happier if this were his biological child. Not until now had the baby felt like a real person to him. Suddenly, this was more than Ashley's child. More than the baby he should have given her long ago. This was a little boy who needed a father, who needed Jarrett.

This was *his* son.

This boy would turn to him for comfort, walk at his side, make him laugh and cry and probably curse. Just as Jarrett had done with his own father. This boy would be a McMullen, a fifth-generation Texan and proud of it.

Jarrett thought the time for quiet thought was over. Ashley needed to marry him. Next week. Sooner, if possible. They needed to proceed with making their family a reality.

He knew better than to start exerting pressure. Ashley had resisted ultimatums and edicts like unbroken ponies fight saddles and reins. Her ordeal and her time away from here had wrought changes in her. She had a maturity and a patience she had not possessed when she left. But she would fight him if he started telling her what she needed to do, what she had to do.

He decided to take a little more subtle approach. He was simply going to assume she had agreed to marry him. The way to start would be tomorrow night, at a holiday party she had agreed to attend with him.

Hosted by the local medical association, the charity benefit would be swarming with friends and colleagues from his medical-school years and beyond.

The doctors from his practice would be there, as well.

The event was perfect for what Jarrett had in mind.

The music and noise from the hotel ballroom boomed into the plush-carpeted hallway. Swamped by sudden uncertainty, Ashley tugged Jarrett to a halt. "Are you sure I look okay?"

He turned with a good-natured sigh. "For about the tenth time this evening, yes, you look beautiful."

"My hair's not too silly?"

He surveyed the upswept curls. "I like it."

Ashley darted a glance toward the elegant dresses of the women who passed them. Sequins flashed. Silk rippled. Satin glowed. Her long, red, crushed-velvet dress was muted by comparison. Her jet earrings and antique choker, which looked so smart at home, paled beside the diamonds and pearls of these women. She groaned. "I look like a big balloon dressed for the high-school prom."

Chuckling, Jarrett kissed her forehead and pulled her forward. "That stomach you keep obsessing about carries my son."

He had been like this ever since the sonogram yesterday afternoon. Positively giddy with the prospect that she was having a boy.

"Sonograms can be wrong, you know," she teased.

He brushed aside that possibility. "You saw it the same as I did. That was no hand, no finger, no nothing but what the tech thought it was. You'd better be thinking up some male names and forget that pink you wanted in the nursery."

In the face of Jarrett's excitement about the baby, Ashley had tried not to worry about his attitude toward her missing memory. Or his real reasons for wanting to marry her. He was full of plans for *their* son, as he referred to the child. Perhaps she was a fool to continue to resist a man so willing to take on a baby sired by someone else.

The line of people entering the ballroom ground to a halt at the big double doors. Someone called Jarrett's name. He turned to greet a big robust-looking fellow with a petite brunette with a friendly smile clinging to his arm.

Jarrett introduced them as Dr. and Mrs. Joseph Cobble. Ashley recognized the name of his biweekly racquetball partner.

"It's Joe to you," the man said, thrusting out his hand. "It's good to finally meet you, Ashley."

"Ashley, this is Steph," Jarrett added. He slipped his arm around Ashley's shoulders. "Steph, this is my fiancée, Ashley Grant."

Fiancée? The term sent Ashley's startled gaze to Jarrett's beaming face. What was he doing?

Now didn't seem to be the time to ask with his friends gushing and carrying on. Steph was pumping her hand and telling her what a good friend Jarrett had been to them.

"We're having a boy," he told Joe.

"You dog." Joe flashed a grin at Ashley. "Steph and I have three girls, and she's not willing to give it another try."

Steph huffed. "You want to try for a boy, you have the baby, Joe Cobble."

She took Ashley's arm as the line moved forward, full of talk about Lamaze classes and pediatricians, breast-feeding versus the bottle. For the next fifteen minutes, Ashley was swallowed up by the Cobbles' natural exuberance.

They were just the start.

Everywhere she and Jarrett turned, he introduced her as his future wife. Those he seemed to know well, he told about the baby being a boy.

Ashley caught some upraised eyebrows. Some speculative glances that lingered on her stomach. One of the doctors from their office looked positively stunned.

But most people were charming. Gracious. Whatever they might be thinking, they kept it to themselves. Many of them appeared to think nothing at all. They assumed the baby was Jarrett's. And he reveled in their congratulations. The only question he kept having to sidestep was the wedding date.

After one such dodge, an older woman gave Jarrett a sharp look. He had introduced her as the head surgeon at the hospital where he had interned. With the familiarity of age and authority, she said, "You marry this woman soon, Dr. McMullen." She turned to Ashley. "The only problem this young man ever had when I was teaching him was his tendency to dillydally. See that he doesn't do that with you and your baby."

She swept away like a queen.

Jarrett burst out laughing. "Now you have to marry me soon, Ashe. Otherwise, she'll be calling me at the office, hounding me at the hospital, probably sending letters to the house."

"You think you're being very slick, don't you?"

All innocence, he looked down at her. "I don't know what you mean."

"Now that you've announced we're getting married, you think I'll just go along with it."

He drew her hand through the crook of his arm. "I confess I thought this might give you a nudge in the right direction."

She pulled her hand away. "I've told you before, Jarrett, I don't like being *handled.*"

He grinned at first, then seemed to finally realize she was dead serious. His smile disappeared. "Ashley, please..."

She turned toward the door. "I want to go home."

While the valet retrieved the Cherokee, Jarrett attempted to apologize. "I'm sorry, Ashley. I'm just tired of waiting. I want to marry you. Why is that a crime?"

"It's not. But blindsiding me the way you did tonight is. I've asked you to be patient. I won't be railroaded. This isn't just your decision alone."

Their vehicle arrived, and they got in. Jarrett's face was set in tight lines and colored with anger. "All right, I know I've screwed up. I'm sorry."

"Fine," Ashley retorted, hoping he would leave it at that for the moment.

But he didn't. "I just want this settled," he said,

"I want to be your husband, the way I should have been a long time ago. I want to claim that baby as my own. I want to put things right, for once and for all."

Put things right. It always came back to duty. To his guilt. No matter how he had gushed about the baby tonight, how proud he had looked when he introduced her as the woman he was going to marry, he was still acting out of guilt.

Oh, he cared for her. He would love this child. But was that enough?

When they arrived at home, she decided it was time they faced the facts.

"I can't marry you, Jarrett," she said. "It's just not right. Not for any of us."

Chapter Eleven

Jarrett stared at Ashley in shock. "Are you going to let what happened tonight keep us apart?"

She headed into the living room, tossing her wrap over one end of the couch. "Tonight is only part of the problem."

"But everything was perfect until I pulled this stunt."

His words struck a dull chord in her. She turned to face him. "That's the problem, isn't it, Jarrett? You want everything to be perfect, and it can't be."

He stepped down from the foyer, frowning. "I don't understand what you mean."

"You want to go back and pretend I never left, that we never hurt each other, that my baby is really yours."

"What's wrong with that?" he demanded. "I'd like to forget everything bad that's ever happened to us."

"But the bad can't be erased. You can't remake me into the person I used to be. You can't use your lasers and your scalpel to put me back together, like you're repairing Toni's face."

"One thing has nothing to do with the other."

"Then tell me what you want to do about my buried past."

"Ignore it."

"But don't you think it will always come rushing back to interfere with us? Until we know the truth, until we can face it, we're crazy to think about going forward."

"I don't believe that for one minute." Jarrett moved toward her again. He said the words he had been pounding at her from the start. "I'm not interested in the past. Just the future. Having you with me again means everything. Having this child with you is the second chance I've wanted ever since I let you get away."

"You *let me*," Ashley repeated. "Once again, you act as if it was all up to you."

"Because I'm the one who messed up."

"No. Maybe it was me. Maybe I was impulsive and silly and I just ran away, thinking you would follow."

He made an impatient gesture. "What does it matter?"

"It matters to me," she insisted. "It's part of my life. Why do you get to choose what's important?"

"I'm just trying to help you see that what we've found together and what we can build is all I care about."

"And what if I care about the truth, about finding out the real answers about the father of my child?"

"I'm the father," Jarrett retorted. "The only father who will ever matter."

"We can't be sure about that."

Jarrett jerked off his black bow tie and peeled out of his tuxedo jacket. "I thought you were starting to put it out of your mind and move forward. I thought you wanted a future with me."

Suddenly cold, she rubbed her arms. "I can't live with my past hanging over us. You want to pretend nothing happened to me."

Hands clenched into fists at his sides, Jarrett muttered a low, emphatic curse. "What you're saying is that you don't trust me to stick by you."

"Oh, you'd stick," she murmured. "You've said over and over again that you're going to prove you can make a commitment to me this time. You're bound and determined to assuage your guilty conscience."

"I'm bound and determined to take care of you."

"Yes, poor, fragile Ashley," she jeered. "She needs someone to care for her. She might run off and disappear into God knows what again. She might fall to pieces. Someone always needs to be around to put her back together."

He made a choppy, dismissive gesture with his hand. "You're not making any sense."

"I'm being irrational?"

He glared at her. "That's not what I said."

"But it's what you think, and you don't like it. You don't want any problems. You want me to be the young, carefree girl I was when we first met."

Jarrett crossed the distance that separated them with three long strides. With restrained force, he took hold of her shoulders and forced her to look at him. "Listen to me, Ashley. Listen close. All I want is for you to be you. The person you are right now. I don't give a damn about anything else. I want you and this child—*our* child. I want us to be a family."

He made it sound so simple, so Norman Rockwell perfect. Ashley didn't believe it was possible. "What happens when *our* son's biological father shows up one day?"

"That's not going to happen."

"You have some guarantee?"

"If it did happen, we could handle it." His hands relaxed on her shoulders. His expression changed from angry to pleading. "Please, Ashley. Give us a chance. Don't close the door because of what might happen."

She searched his lean, handsome features for several moments. "What about the door to my past, Jarrett? Do you want that closed instead?"

"I can't control that."

"But you would if you could. Admit it."

He let go of her and turned around, one hand lifting to thrust through his dark hair. The room was silent until he spoke. "All right," he muttered, still not facing her. "I'll admit it. I don't want you to remember."

Ashley hugged her arms to her chest as she gazed at his bent head.

"I don't want anyone else to try and claim your baby, *my* son." The breath he sucked in was ragged. "But most of all..."

He turned, his dark eyes bright with tears. "Most of all, I don't want to know some other man succeeded where I failed you. I don't want to hear that you loved him."

The dejection in his voice and his posture nearly broke her heart. Ashley reached out to him, stepped into his arms and held on.

Low against her ear, he whispered, "Let's not worry about what we don't know. Marry me, Ashe. Be happy. I know it's the best for both of us."

Those words were like a sledgehammer. They smashed into the wall in her mind and a split appeared. Ashley jerked away from Jarrett, staring at him in disbelief. Suddenly, she was eighteen again, and Jarrett was murmuring that same pat phrase as they agreed to call off their wedding.

I know it's best for both of us.

He had ripped her heart in two with those words. Torn her life apart. That's why she ran away.

The memories returned like a leap into the unknown. One moment she was struggling through the pull of the familiar. Then she burst into the blank space. A space filled with all her mind had tried to destroy.

That rathole of an apartment in California.

The endless rounds of temporary jobs.

Loneliness.

And fear like a black cloak.

She remembered the few phone calls she had allowed herself to make home. All the lies she had told her family about how happy she was, how many friends she was making, what a great life she was going to have on the coast.

Gray had never sounded like he was buying the act. He made her so furious she stopped calling. She vowed not to contact her family again until she could truthfully say she was doing well.

The struggle not to call Jarrett had been worst of all.

She had wanted him there. She had needed him. But she knew if she gave in, she would crawl back home. She would live by his timetable. Let him make all the decisions in her life. And she couldn't do that.

Perhaps it was inevitable that she had drifted into a relationship with the first man who was kind to her.

His name had been Rob.

With that name, she was suddenly drawing blanks again.

Ashley looked up, surprised to see Jarrett was simply standing there, staring at her. She felt as if she had been on a long journey. Had all of this really returned in the blink of an eye?

"Are you okay?" Concern tightened his features.

After the feelings he had just confessed, Ashley didn't see how she could tell him the memories that were filtering back. Yet wasn't that pretending, as he wanted? Wasn't that hiding from the truth she claimed they needed to find?

She squared her shoulders and faced Jarrett. "I've remembered something. A man."

Jarrett's lips thinned.

"His name was Rob," she whispered. "Rob Walters."

The silence was thick enough to cut.

"The baby's father?" Jarrett asked, his voice husky.

"I don't know." Misery sent scalding tears to her eyes. "Oh, damnation! Why don't I know? What's wrong with me that I can't remember?" She pressed both hands to her head. "It's all right here, Jarrett. I can feel it. Why can't I remember?"

He took her hands into his. "Stop it now. Settle down. Take a deep breath."

She mindlessly obeyed his commands. All the while, her mind was racing, searching through the twists and turns of her life, finding clear sailing until she thought of Rob, and she crashed and burned.

Could Rob be somewhere, waiting for her?

She had to know, but nothing came to her.

She could feel Jarrett's unease. If was as if his worst nightmare had been conjured by his words.

Eventually, Jarrett insisted they turn in. He promised that tomorrow they would call the Canadian authorities who had worked on her case to see if Rob's name meant anything.

Ashley went to bed, but she barely slept. Jarrett was called to the hospital the next morning on an emergency. While he was gone, more bits and pieces of her missing years filtered back.

She remembered Rob as a gentle loner. Not really handsome. But with soulful green eyes and a tender smile. He was Canadian, and about her age. His parents had died when he was teenager, leaving him to fend for himself. He had drifted to the States, working construction, mostly, where he was paid in cash and no one asked too many questions about green cards and work releases. She met him when she worked a temporary job at a builder's office. He had loved Italian food, the mountains in the winter...and her.

The memory of his sad, hopeless love triggered the next onslaught in Ashley. She had never been able to love him with all her heart. She had loved Jarrett, still.

But Rob needed her, wanted her.

She agreed when Rob asked her to travel with him. They both found cash jobs in California, Oregon and Washington, which explained why no one who tried to trace her had been able to pick up a trail. Eventually, Rob wanted to go home. He had heard of steady work with a mining company that had employed him before. The pay was extremely good. Ashley had agreed. Their plan was to save enough for a move to Hawaii.

They ended up in a cold, dismal town just north of Edmonton in Alberta. The weather turned cold and bleak early on. The snow started in August. Everyone kept to themselves. There was no job for Ashley. She had felt like an outsider, the American girl with the strange accent.

Time and again, she considered leaving. She yearned for her family. She knew they must be worried sick, that she was hurting them. But what could she tell them if she called? *Send money? Come and get me?*

She clung to her pride like a captain going down with his ship. Even after she discovered Rob had gambled most of his money on a get-rich-quick scheme that backfired.

Ashley wasn't sure how she made it through. It helped that Rob was so kind to her. He thought she was beautiful. He brought her little gifts, left cards where she would find them in their small trailer. Every minute he wasn't working was dedicated to her. She thought she needed his adoration, even if she couldn't return it. She was afraid she would never be lucky enough to find another man who loved her this much.

And yet she wanted to go home. For the final months in that dreary place, Ashley was working up enough courage to get out, to leave Rob.

Had he sensed it and tried to stop her? Ashley couldn't conceive of him being violent with her.

But what had happened?

He loved her. So how had she ended up dazed and

alone on a street well south and west of where they lived?

The authorities might be able to trace her steps, tell her what had happened to Rob, but what would that mean if she didn't remember herself? For months, she had listened to tales of her life without feeling any connection at all. She wasn't going to wait for these answers. She had to go back to that dreary little town, to find out for herself.

Jarrett would have a fit if she suggested such a thing. Gray would, too. They would do everything they could to stop her, to convince her she wasn't being smart or logical. She wasn't going to give them a chance.

Pausing only to pack a small bag, she scribbled a note to Jarrett. She couldn't go off without telling him where she might be found, not after disappearing before.

At the airport, she was lucky enough to find a flight leaving soon. The ticket cost her every dime she had saved toward the baby's nursery. But her peace of mind was more important than white wicker and a layette.

Within two hours of making her decision to leave, her jet was flying north. By this time the next day, she might have her answers.

Jarrett nearly lost his mind when he came home and found Ashley's note. A frantic call to the airport revealed she was indeed aboard a plane bound to Seattle, with a connecting flight to Edmonton. She was going to some godforsaken little town in Alberta, Canada, in order to find this man she had lived with. This Rob Walters.

He couldn't bear to think that she might be fleeing to be with this Rob. He couldn't accept that she might have remembered she loved this other man.

Jarrett felt he had to follow her. He couldn't let her walk away, perhaps disappear again.

He called Greta and put her in charge of clearing his schedule and finding someone to cover for him for the next few days. Then he headed for the airport.

It was midnight before he got to Seattle, and the next connecting flight wasn't until early the next morning. He slept at the airport and arrived in cold, snow-covered Edmonton.

A car-rental agent remembered Ashley because of her accent and her pregnancy. She had left the airport late last night, with the town she had mentioned in her note given as her destination. The agent said it was about a three-hour drive.

Jarrett rented a car and set out after her. The roads were clear, but still treacherous with ice in spots. With each curve, he expected to find a car overturned in a ditch, Ashley inside. It was late afternoon when he reached the town called Red Lake.

There was not much to it. A mining-company office. A cluster of rusted mobile homes and small houses. A run-down motel. A grocery and dry-goods store. A post office and a row of assorted other businesses. Two bars and a restaurant.

Jarrett started in the latter and struck pay dirt. The

man presiding over the premises from behind a long counter had talked to Ashley just a few hours before.

"She came in, looking for information about the Walters boy who died in that accident last summer."

At first Jarrett thought he was just loopy from weariness. "Did you say Rob Walters is dead?"

The man nodded. "It was a head-on collision last June. He was on his way home from the mine, and it was foggy...." He shook his head. "Like I told the woman, the poor bastard didn't have a chance."

While Jarrett absorbed this information, the man paused, stroking his unshaved jaw. "I've been thinking about that woman ever since she left. She looks a lot like the girl that Walters fella lived with, but she didn't act like she knew anything about the accident."

Jarrett grunted impatiently. "Do you know where she went?"

The stranger shrugged. "Maybe to the motel. She looked about done in."

With a quick thank-you tossed over his shoulder, Jarrett headed back up the street to the Red Lake Inn. The parking lot was empty, but the clerk at the front desk remembered Ashley, too. She had asked where to find the local cemetery.

And that's where Jarrett found her. Wrapped in a long black coat that he didn't recognize, she was standing beside a grave that sported a fresh sheaf of flowers.

As he drew near, Jarrett could hear her crying.

He thought his heart would explode.

He walked closer, his shoes crunching through the blanket of snow, but Ashley didn't look up. Her attention was focused on the tiny plot of land where the man she had come to find was buried.

Obviously, she must have loved him.

The man was dead, but Jarrett's insides still twisted with envy. The worst of all possible scenarios had come true.

He came to a stop a few steps behind Ashley. A cold wind rattled through the bare branches of the tree overhead. The sound was as forlorn as Jarrett felt.

So it had all come down to this. Ashley had been right to think Jarrett feared her past. He feared this moment of loss.

For most of the years that Ashley had been gone, he had told himself he hadn't really lost her. He had been certain if she came home, if they found her, she would be his again. To protect. To cherish. To never let go again. That knowledge, that certainty, had kept him from moving on in any real sense. Had kept him looking for her everywhere he went.

But it seemed she *had* moved on. To someone else. A man she was mourning now. A man whose child she carried.

The pain inside Jarrett was as sharp as the bitterly cold air he drew into his lungs. It hurt to know Ashley loved someone else. But it didn't change the way he felt. He loved her still. Would love her always.

Ashley spoke, and Jarrett strained to hear her words. "I'm sorry, Rob. So sorry."

Then she turned around and immediately stepped back in surprise. One black-gloved hand fluttered to her face. "Jarrett, what are you doing here?"

His throat was too clogged with emotion to speak.

"I found Rob," Ashley said unnecessarily.

"And all your memories," Jarrett forced out.

She nodded. "I couldn't wait to call the authorities and let them check things out. I had to know. See this firsthand."

They stared at each other across that frozen stretch of ground.

Stepping closer, Jarrett studied her face. She was pale from the cold. Tears were drying in icy patches on her cheeks. For all her sadness, there was something in her expression, something…free. That was the only way he could explain what he saw.

And why shouldn't she have that peace? She had the answers she had sought. Tragic though the explanation might be, the blank spaces in her mind were now filled in.

Finally, Jarrett cleared his throat. "I'm sorry, Ashley. Sorry he's gone."

In flat, nearly emotionless tones, she gave him a brief account of how she and this man had come to this place and the accident that had claimed his life.

With every fiber of his being, Jarrett wanted to tell her he didn't care about this man, that he loved her and wanted her to marry him. Yet what an insult that would be. To try to pretend this man hadn't existed would be to negate a part of her life. Negate the father of her baby. Jarrett couldn't do that.

His instincts were to try to take over. Sweep her away. Try to make up for her loss, try to make her forget. But then he would be the man she had accused him of being. Someone who wanted to dictate her decisions, her feelings. He saw he couldn't do that any longer. He couldn't force Ashley to bend to his will. Not as he had done from the very first, when they were just kids.

Maybe that was part of the problem. They fell in love so young, when they were both immature and certainly not ready for the responsibilities of commitment. Even later, when they tried to get back together, he had viewed her as flighty and irresponsible, someone he had to take charge of. Instead of walking with her, he wanted to lead. Ashley deserved better.

"I owe you an apology," Jarrett told her. "I've been hardheaded where you're concerned."

She looked surprised. "Please, Jarrett. Don't cast yourself as an ogre. You've also been very kind and encouraging."

"But I was every bit as afraid of your past as you thought I was. I did want to make up for what happened, you know. I did want to go back to the way things were. I know now that no one can really do that, but I did want to try."

Ashley took a step forward. She couldn't stand seeing the devastation in his face. "Stop it, please. For once and for all, none of what happened to me was all your fault. Or all mine." She glanced back at the grave. "No one's fault."

"Was he good to you, Ashe?" Jarrett's voice was rough with emotion.

"He was better than I deserved," she whispered.

Jarrett nodded, though he made no comment. His next words surprised her. "What do you want to do now?"

She would have expected him to have a plan. To present it to her. She swallowed hard. "I want to go home."

"To Gray's, I guess."

Her eyes widened, but she made no protest. Amarillo no longer felt like home.

Perhaps he read that in her expression. "It's up to you, Ashley. Whatever you want."

She managed a short laugh. "Isn't it strange? For most of my life, I've just wanted to make my own decisions without anyone else's interference. That's why I took off. When you decided to play the boss with me, just like Gray always had, I just couldn't take it any longer. But then I messed up pretty good. Now I think I'm afraid to make a choice."

"Afraid?" Jarrett shook his head. "You're anything but a coward, Ashe. Whatever else this whole experience brought you, whatever problems, it also made you stronger."

His words stunned her. "You think I'm strong?"

"Of course. How else have you coped since coming to in the hospital, being told you were expecting a child and not knowing who you were? You always had a core of strength as tough as buffalo hide. I knew that. My problem was in not respecting that toughness.''

She was amazed. Somewhere in the vast jumble of these past two days, Jarrett had acquired some important insights. Yet she honestly couldn't gauge exactly what he was feeling for her. He looked at her as if she were a stranger.

She had to try, however. "I have to tell you everything that happened, Jarrett. All about me and Rob.''

He set his jaw, looking as if he'd sooner take a dive off a cliff than hear this. But he said, "All right.''

"I didn't know I was pregnant when he died,'' she murmured. "But once I realized that, I wrapped things up around here real fast. I had to get out of here, out of this horrible town. I had a little money, not much after burying Rob and paying off our bills. But I thought I might find a job in Seattle while I decided what I was going to do.''

"But you never made it to Seattle?''

"I had to change buses in that town where I ended up in the hospital.'' She shook her head. "There was a layover. I was going to get something to eat. It was dark. I remember someone walking up beside me. The next thing I knew, I was in that hospital where you found me.''

"You were mugged, just like they said.''

"But even before that, I was in a fog.'' She fought back her tears again. "All I wanted was to come home, Jarrett. I had wanted that for so long. Even

before Rob died. Before the baby. I remembered
thinking I had screwed up my whole life and now I
was having a baby.''

''Surely you weren't sad about the baby? It was
his baby, after all.''

Ashley gazed at him in confusion. ''What do you
mean?''

He had to push the words out. ''The baby of the
man you loved. Surely that wasn't so horrible.''

She stepped forward, her hand outstretched.
''That's just it, Jarrett. I didn't love him.''

He shook his head, not certain he had heard her
correctly.

''I loved you, Jarrett. I always loved you. Even
when I was with him. When he died...'' She put her
hand to her lips to quiet a sob. ''He was dead, and
all I could think about was getting home and seeing
you. I wanted you back, Jarrett. I never ever stopped
wanting you and just you.''

''But you were crying at his grave, Ashley. I heard
you, saw you.''

''He was a good man. But I didn't do right by
him. I should have left and come home. I should have
found you. But I didn't. I stayed with him, out of
guilt. Out of obligation. And then he died. He was
dead, and I knew I had made him so unhappy, because he knew I didn't love him the way I should.''

She closed her eyes, reliving the torture of those
feelings. Emotions she was so afraid Jarrett would
now apply to her. She couldn't let him.

''And then you were pregnant,'' Jarrett prompted.

"And I wanted to find you. But I didn't think you could accept me or the baby. I thought you would be horrified by my pregnancy."

Joy was breaking inside Jarrett like a sunrise. He reached out and took Ashley in his arms. "But now you know," he whispered. "You know I'm not horrified." Through her thick coat, he stroked her stomach. "In all the ways that matter, this is *my* child. I've loved you since the moment I met you, and there isn't any way I couldn't love a child who is a part of you."

She gave him a searching look. "You don't owe me anything, Jarrett. You know that, don't you?"

"I owe you my love," he insisted. "Because that's what is in my heart. It's the truth. It always has been."

Believing him was easy. The proof shone in his eyes. With a cry of joy, she lifted her lips to his.

"Love brought us back together," Ashley murmured when she drew away. "It lived on when my mind shut down. That's how I knew your name when you walked into the hospital room."

"Love will get us through everything." He touched her stomach again. "All of us."

Epilogue

On an unseasonably warm afternoon in mid-February, after ten hours of labor, after an entire extended family flew into Dallas, Ashley gave birth to her son. A whopping nine-and-a-half pound baby boy with dark hair and her golden-hued eyes.

Well after the delivery, when she had celebrated with all the aunts and uncles and cousins and grandparents, when everyone had oohed and aahed until they were almost as exhausted as she, Ashley watched her husband hold their little boy.

She couldn't help think of Rob. She hoped she could make this child understand how much Rob would have loved him. But she was eternally grateful her son would have Jarrett.

"He's going to be a great kid," Jarrett said, looking up at her with the giddy smile of a newly minted father.

"Robert Gray McMullen." The name, chosen by Jarrett, felt good on Ashley's lips.

"Let's just call him Rob," Jarrett suggested, looking at his son instead of her. "It fits a little guy, don't you think?"

Touched beyond measure, Ashley had to swallow her tears. What a rare, special man her husband was. A man who had held on to his love for her beyond all reason. A man who loved and would raise another man's child like his own.

"Rob is a very good name," Ashley agreed when she could finally speak. Her gaze met her husband's and clung—warm with a love and respect that deepened every day.

Ashley had become the woman she had always wanted to be. A woman who could think for herself, but knew when she needed her partner, as well. But then, Jarrett, the man who used to try to tame her, made it easy for her to be herself.

With a happy sigh, she held out her arms for her baby. "Right now, everything in my life fits just right. Thank you, Dr. McMullen."

"Thank you," Jarrett replied, his heart full. "For your love. And for giving me my perfect little boy."

As if he approved, young Rob grabbed his father's thumb and wouldn't let go.

* * * * *

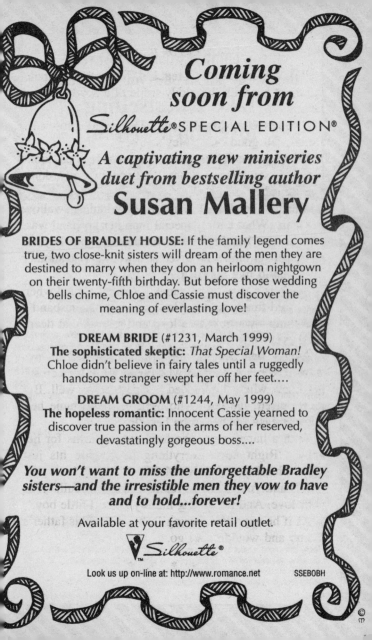

Coming soon from

Silhouette ® SPECIAL EDITION ®

A captivating new miniseries duet from bestselling author
Susan Mallery

BRIDES OF BRADLEY HOUSE: If the family legend comes true, two close-knit sisters will dream of the men they are destined to marry when they don an heirloom nightgown on their twenty-fifth birthday. But before those wedding bells chime, Chloe and Cassie must discover the meaning of everlasting love!

DREAM BRIDE (#1231, March 1999)
The sophisticated skeptic: *That Special Woman!*
Chloe didn't believe in fairy tales until a ruggedly handsome stranger swept her off her feet....

DREAM GROOM (#1244, May 1999)
The hopeless romantic: Innocent Cassie yearned to discover true passion in the arms of her reserved, devastatingly gorgeous boss....

You won't want to miss the unforgettable Bradley sisters—and the irresistible men they vow to have and to hold...forever!

Available at your favorite retail outlet.

Silhouette ®

If you enjoyed what you just read,
then we've got an offer you can't resist!

Take 2 bestselling love stories FREE!

Plus get a FREE surprise gift!

Silhouette® SPECIAL EDITION®

presents **THE BRIDAL CIRCLE,** a brand-new
miniseries honoring friendship, family and love...

THE BRIDAL CIRCLE

by

Andrea Edwards

They dreamed of marrying and leaving their
small town behind—but soon discovered there's
no place like home for true love!

IF I ONLY HAD A...HUSBAND (May '99)
Penny Donnelly had tried desperately to forget charming
millionaire Brad Corrigan. But her heart had a memory—and a
will—of its own. And Penny's heart was set on Brad becoming
her husband....

SECRET AGENT GROOM (August '99)
When shy-but-sexy Heather Mahoney bumbles onto secret agent
Alex Waterstone's undercover mission, the only way to protect the
innocent beauty is to claim her as his lady love. Will Heather
carry out her own secret agenda and claim Alex as her groom?

PREGNANT & PRACTICALLY MARRIED
(November '99)
Pregnant Karin Spencer had suddenly lost her memory and
gained a pretend fiancé. Though their match was make-believe,
Jed McCarron was her dream man. Could this bronco-bustin'
cowboy give up his rodeo days for family ways?

Available at your favorite retail outlet.

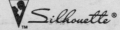

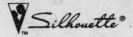

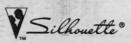

HARLEQUIN *Duets*™

2 new full-length novels by
2 great authors in
1 book for 1 low price!

Buy any Harlequin Duets™ book
and **SAVE $1.00!**

SAVE $1.00

when you purchase any

 HARLEQUIN

Duets™ book!

Offer valid May 1, 1999, to October 31, 1999.

HDUETC-U

 HARLEQUIN®
Makes any time special.™

**Coupon expires
October 31, 1999.**

5 65373 00051 9   (8100) 1 06254

HARLEQUIN *Duets*™

2 new full-length novels by 2 great authors in 1 book for 1 low price!

Buy any Harlequin Duets™ book and **SAVE $1.00!**

SAVE $1.00

when you purchase any

 HARLEQUIN

Duets™ book!

Offer valid May 1, 1999, to October 31, 1999.

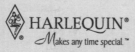 **HARLEQUIN**®
Makes any time special.™

HDUETC-C

**Coupon expires
October 31, 1999.**
